Praise for *Lucky Breaks*

"With sensitivity and precision, Patron delves into the complexities surrounding friendship. . . . Return readers will be contented to once again pass some time in Hard Pan, while those like Paloma, who are new to the community, will feel embraced by its close-knit (or should that be close-*knot*?) warmth."—*Horn Book Magazine*

"In this fully satisfying sequel, Lucky continues to be the sturdy character a reader can believe in—prone to what one might quaintly call 'scrapes,' but bright and big-hearted in the tradition of Anne Shirley and Jo March."—*Bulletin of the Center for Children's Books*

"[Rides] the same wave of warmth and quirkiness that distinguished Patron's Newbery–winning *The Higher Power of Lucky* . . . [Patron] skillfully balances sentimentality and humor, allowing her characters to shine once more in their own idiosyncratic ways."
—*Publishers Weekly*

"Lucky's world [is] a charmer of a place. . . . Unusual metaphors, vivid language, felicitous writing, and the sense of hearing from a realistic, albeit unique child are the strengths that continue in this sequel that is as tightly plotted as the first book."—*School Library Journal*

"Patron nails the insecurities and overzealousness of a budding friendship."—*Booklist*

 lucky breaks

Also by Susan Patron

The Higher Power of Lucky

Maybe Yes, Maybe No, Maybe Maybe

lucky breaks

by **susan patron**

with illustrations by matt phelan

Atheneum Books for Young Readers
New York London Toronto Sydney

ATHENEUM BOOKS FOR YOUNG READERS
An imprint of Simon & Schuster Children's Publishing Division
1230 Avenue of the Americas
New York, New York 10020

This book is a work of fiction. Any references to historical events, real people, or real locales are used fictitiously. Other names, characters, places, and incidents are products of the author's imagination, and any resemblance to actual events or locales or persons, living or dead, is entirely coincidental.

For information about special discounts for bulk purchases, please contact Simon & Schuster Special Sales at 1-866-506-1949 or business@simonandschuster.com.
The Simon & Schuster Speakers Bureau can bring authors to your live event. For more information or to book an event, contact the Simon & Schuster Speakers Bureau at 1-866-248-3049 or visit our website at www.simonspeakers.com.
Also available in an Atheneum Books for Young Readers hardcover edition.
Book design by Sonia Chaghatzbanian
The text for this book is set in Berkeley.
The illustrations for this book are rendered in pen, ink, and pencil.
Manufactured in the United States of America
0410 OFF
First Atheneum Books for Young Readers paperback edition May 2010
10 9 8 7 6 5 4 3 2 1
The Library of Congress has cataloged the hardcover edition as follows:
Patron, Susan.
Lucky breaks / by Susan Patron ; with illustrations by Matt Phelan.—1st ed.
p. cm.
Sequel: The higher power of Lucky.
Summary: Having reached the mature age of eleven in the tiny California town of Hard Pan (population 43), Lucky discovers that there is still much to learn about friendship, parental trust, and the Milky Way galaxy.
Includes bibliographical references (p. 181)
ISBN: 978-1-4169-3998-6 (hc)
[1. Friendship—Fiction. 2. Interpersonal relations—Fiction. 3. Adoption—Fiction. 4. Abandoned children—Fiction. 5. Deserts—Fiction. 6. California—Fiction.] I. Phelan, Matt, ill. II. Title.
PZ7.P27565Lu 2009
[Fic]—dc22 2008051440
ISBN 978-1-4169-9772-6 (pbk)
ISBN 978-1-4391-6376-4 (eBook)

For René, *toujours*

contents

1. a broken brooch

Eleven, Lucky thought from her seat at the back of the school bus, *eleven, eleven, eleven*, and the idea of it, the sound of it, threw off sparks in her head. You start with one, two, three: those clunky one-syllable beginner-ages like wooden blocks that toddlers play with. Keep going and you get to eight, nine, ten: the plodding steps you have to climb until, at last, you arrive. Finally, finally, you reach the best age, the one that, when you say it out loud, sounds like a little tap dance or a drumroll.

And now Lucky was almost there, about to turn eleven, a dazzling change. Not the thud of ten, but flouncy e-lev-en, with its sophisticated three syllables. Write it as numerals and you have a pair of ones, side by side; a fearless two-part beginning, the door to becoming a teenager. She pictured 11 as a swinging double door, a saloon door in an old Western; you push the sides open, *bam*, with both hands and stride through before they flap shut again, your childhood behind you. And her secret 11: the two straps of Lucky's brand-new bra, her first.

As the whole miraculousness of eleven sparked in Lucky's brain, the big bus with its three passengers in the very back seat jolted along the highway toward Sierra City; it was the last day of the first week of school. Lincoln, smelling of pencil lead, frowned over a complicated, much-creased diagram; it looked like the pattern for an intricate weaving of some kind and was accompanied by numbers and letters of different colors. Lincoln didn't seem to have changed when he turned eleven half a year ago; he still tied knots, always practicing and learning new ones. Miles, by the window, clutched a bubble-wrapped object in his small, grimy hands.

2   "Lucky," Miles said, leaning forward to peer around Lincoln's diagram, "look at my show-and-tell. It's a wing!"

Lincoln raised his paper without taking his eyes off it, allowing Lucky to reach across for the object. But Miles jerked back. "Nobody can touch it," he said, "because it's from the Found Object Wind Chime Museum, and Short Sammy said I should borrow it because my only other show-and-tell was a piece of vacuum hose, but I had to promise no one would touch it, even Miss B."

"Well, I can't really see it, Miles. You've got it all covered up with bubble wrap."

"Yeah, so I'll do the 'tell' part now and the 'show' part when the bus stops, and you can look close but you still can't touch it."

Lucky knew that Miles took his responsibilities very seriously, for a five-going-on-six-year-old. "Okay," she agreed.

"Okay," Miles echoed happily, settling back into his seat, cradling his object.

After a minute, Lincoln folded his diagram and said, "So what is the 'tell' part? What did you mean, that it's a wing?"

"Oh, yeah," Miles said. "It's part of a brooch that got shot in half by a miner called Burro Bob about a hundred years ago. You probably don't know what a brooch is. It's a pin."

"A pin?" Lucky asked.

"Yeah, like jewelry. Ladies wear them on their"—Miles's cheeks suddenly turned deep red—"here." He pointed a dirty-looking finger at his chest. "So this woman, her name was Paloma, got killed by a bullet right in her heart. She got fought over by two miners, Burro Bob and his partner, Frank the Fuse. Anyway, her name means 'dove' in Spanish, and that's why Burro Bob made the pin in the shape of a dove. He made it out of garnets and quartz and some other thing, I think amnesia, all from mines around Hard Pan."

One corner of Lincoln's mouth twitched at the word "amnesia," a tiny smile Lucky knew was meant for her, but not Miles, to see.

"And Bob and his burro were digging this well for water, only they never found any. But Frank tried to take Paloma for himself, so Bob plugged him"—Miles formed his hand as if it were a gun, aimed at the front of the bus, pulled the trigger, made the sound of a gunshot, and fell back in his seat from the recoil— "but somehow the bullet got Paloma instead." Miles jumped up to enact the part of the wounded Paloma, making agonized death sounds while clutching his chest to stop the bleeding.

"Get back in your seat, Miles!" Sandi the bus driver shouted from the front.

Miles slid onto his seat, still dying. "I *am* in my seat!" he shouted back.

"So," said Lucky, "she died?"

"Yeah. The bullet went right through the brooch and got her in the heart. It broke the pin in two. Sammy says the piece they found"—Miles held up the wrapped object—"is the wing of the dove, and the rest of the brooch is at the bottom of the well, which was—what's it called when they give up and quit working, like at a mine, and close it?"

"Abandoned," Lincoln said. "Or condemned."

"Yeah, abandoned." Miles carefully slid the bubble-wrap-covered pin into an empty plastic Band-Aid box, snapping the lid shut. "Burro Bob and Frank the Fuse disappeared and never got caught, but Short Sammy says lots of people have tried to find the rest of the dove brooch, its head and stuff, by climbing down into the old well."

"Abandoned or condemned," Lucky repeated softly, thinking how sad those words sounded, how lonely. They could be words about wells, and they could also be words about people.

"They should seal up those old wells," Lincoln said, gazing out the window. "They're dangerous." His mother had named him Lincoln Clinton Carter Kennedy because she wanted him to grow up to be the president of the United States. Lucky noticed that he often looked and sounded like a future president, grave and serious and diplomatic. She remembered when they were only seven and she teased him to make him chase her, then tripped and fell smack on her chin. The bright red gush of her own blood on the ground scared her. Lincoln had yanked off his T-shirt and pressed it hard against her chin. "Stay put and keep pressing," he'd said before going for help, already talking in that presidential way. And Lucky ended up with a little three-stitch scar on the underside of her chin, a scar like a tiny upside-down *L*.

Miles looked at them. "Anyway," he said. "There's bloody murder and no kissing, so it's a good show-and-tell story."

When they got off the bus, they piled their backpacks on a bench and Miles opened his Band-Aid box, slid the bubble wrap out, and very carefully unrolled it. Lucky, more interested in the museum's bugs and birds, had never noticed the little piece of jewelry. She bent over the mosaic of gems, bordered by a band of silver in a wing shape, intricate and beautiful.

"Wow," Lucky said as Miles rewrapped the pin and put it back into the box. "I wish we could see the rest of the brooch. Imagine the glory if we found it ourselves."

Lincoln frowned. "Don't even think about it," he said.

"Yeah," Miles said, the worry about the dangerousness of abandoned wells on his face. "Forget about it, Lucky."

But Lucky was considering how, when you're eleven, you're interested in love and murder, blood and glory and kissing, things that are precious and fragile, things that are abandoned or condemned. Because eleven is much more intrepid than only ten.

2. a secret

"Lincoln," Brigitte said in her tired-feet voice from inside the kitchen trailer. "First, push that little stool over here so I can get my feet up. Then you will tell me what is this big knot project that you carry everywhere in the black sack."

Just outside, squatting in the wedge of shade cast by an A-frame sign, Lucky listened through the open windows. In a cheerful welcoming curlicue way the sign's bright red letters said:

Brigitte's Hard Pan Café
Open for
Lunch/Déjeuner
Sat—Sun & Holidays

So before the weekend when she would be busy helping Brigitte, Lucky was searching for worms on a row of potted tomato plants that bordered the little cluster of Café tables and chairs. Part keen-eyed hunter, part keen-eared listener, she, too, wondered about Lincoln's secret project, which he carried slung over his shoulder in a big Santa Clausy sack. Except Santa didn't carry his stuff in an extra-large, heavy-duty black plastic trash bag the way Lincoln did.

"It's for a contest," Lincoln said, "of the International Guild of Knot Tyers."

Lucky already knew that much. She herself had tried to pry the secret of what the thing actually *was* out of Lincoln, but he wouldn't tell. Lucky had her own private theory about it but hoped she was wrong. Lincoln had a doofus-dorky side that was kind of sweet, but there were limits. She couldn't believe that he would spend weeks making a fishing net. Not in the middle of the Mojave Desert, where there wasn't an ocean for zillions of miles around. However, each time Lucky had stolen a glimpse of the thing in the black plastic trash bag, it had always looked exactly like . . . a fishing net.

Lucky examined the underside of a large stem, sniffing its unripe-tomato smell.

Lucky would have liked to probe into the compartment of Lincoln's brain where he kept his secrets, using one of those special scientific-medical instruments that have a teeny tiny camera on the very end. In some ways she felt that she already knew quite a lot of what was in his brain, but lately he'd become sort of different—not older, exactly, but a little bit more reserved. Without knowing exactly why, Lucky worried about this slight and gradual change in Lincoln, and she hated not knowing the particular secret about whatever he was making for the knot contest.

At least she did know the secret of tomato worms, which is camouflage. Since they are *exactly* the same color green as tomato leaves and stems, and since their bodies have little angular notches to resemble branches, they look just like part of the tomato plant and are hard to see. Lucky understood about creatures blending in with their habitat because she herself had skin, eyes, and hair exactly the color of the sand and rocks of Hard Pan, California, where she lived. But she had seen the all-time best example of an animal camouflaging itself on a program recently: caterpillars in Japan that looked exactly like bird droppings! Lucky pictured the whole thing: the predators going, "Eww, don't eat those—they're bird droppings!" while the caterpillars lie around laughing. Her hero, Charles Darwin, had been dead for way over a hundred years, but she knew he'd love the caterpillar story, and she held a little conversation with him in her mind, telling him the whole thing.

Her worm-hunting technique had to do with the fact that tomato worms go to the bathroom just like everyone else. So she put white paper on the soil underneath where branches stuck out from the barrel. Eventually little black dots appeared on the paper, which meant there was a tomato worm directly above. The black dots were his droppings. So then you made your eyes

9

travel all along every branch and leaf above those black dots, very carefully and thoroughly, especially on the underneath sides—and sooner or later, if you were patient, you'd spot the worm.

As Lucky searched, she heard Brigitte say from inside the kitchen trailer, "And if you are winning that contest, then perhaps you will go to the headquarters in England for the big convention of the Knot Tyers?"

"Well," Lincoln said, "yeah, but it's even better than that. I'd go to England, and one guy who's been helping me, Mr. Budworth, he's the best knot tyer alive—he's written more than a dozen books on knotting—he and his wife offered to put me up for the summer, that's how they say it over there, 'We'll put you up,' so I'd have a place to stay for free. Mr. Budworth knows *everything*; he knows the entire history of knots, and how the same knot will show up in different countries. He says I could help him with *Knotting Matters*, which is even more cool than *Knot News*; it's got articles and stories by knotters from all over the world. Going to England is really why I want to win the contest. My dad says if I do win, he'll pay for the plane ticket. *Plus*—" Lincoln broke off.

"Plus what?" Brigitte asked.

"Well, Mrs. Budworth wants me to stay on with them and go to school in England for a year. She says I need much more challenge than I'm getting here, and she thinks I'd love the school where their own kids went."

A bad feeling came over Lucky. The thought of Lincoln being gone next year, or even just for the summer, made her stop hunting worms and sit back on the ground, not caring about getting the seat of her jeans gritty. Lincoln would become this contest-winning world traveler, meeting all sorts of interesting people, living in a real city with the most famous knot-man in the world, probably skipping a grade when he finally came back home because he'd be so far ahead of everyone here. And Lucky herself would be . . . abandoned. *And* condemned; condemned to a bleak, lonely life, without—without any other person her own age in Hard Pan.

And that was when a thought like a gas bubble in the La Brea Tar Pits seeped up, murky and foul. The thought had to do with Lincoln somehow *not* winning that contest. It came from Lucky's anxiety gland, which could get overactive. She forced herself to concentrate on tomato worms.

Inside, Brigitte and Lincoln had begun to discuss food. Lucky knew that a bunch of geologists had made a reservation at the Café for lunch on Saturday, and Brigitte had told Lincoln about the soups and salads and sandwiches on her menu. She'd just asked Lincoln if there were something else he thought geologists would like.

"Hamburgers," said Lincoln.

"Ah, *non*," Brigitte said, but not in her tired-feet voice. This was her I-won't-change-my-mind voice. "They can get their hamburgers anyplace. The Hard Pan Café does not have them. The Café is a little bit Californian, but also it is a little bit French, and that is why people like to come. But never, never, never do I cook the hamburger."

They had had this conversation before. There were even a bunch of Hard Pan advisers helping Brigitte with her studies to become an American citizen. She wanted, she said, to learn the kinds of things that they don't have on the test, things that would make her more like a *real* Californian. The advisors included Lincoln, Lucky, Miles, Short Sammy, Dot, the Captain, and actually just about all forty-three residents of Hard Pan. Most of them had told Brigitte, in addition to other tips, that she should serve hamburgers at the Café. So Brigitte practiced making the *th* sound, which she said was very hard for people with French tongues, and she tried to understand the rules of baseball, and she learned how to turn avocados into guacamole. But to hamburgers on her menu, she always firmly said *non*.

3. delicious little animals

Lucky spotted a worm, a big soft fat one. The word for not wanting to touch a big soft fat worm is squeamish, which has a built-in sound of exactly the feeling in your fingers as they reach for that worm. Being, like Charles Darwin, a scientist, Lucky un-squeamished her fingers. Worms grasp their branch strongly, so you have to get a really firm grip on their bodies in order to pry them off.

She didn't kill the worms, first because they were gooshy and mushy and she did not want to see them bleed; second because she was fine with protecting the tomatoes from them but at the same time she was not a cold-blooded worm murderer; and third because she was saving them in a jar as a present for the Captain's chickens. Most of the old LUSCIOUS TOMATOES label was still on the jar, so in a funny way it was exactly right for a temporary tomato worm home.

The Captain's chickens loved tomato worms, and once Lucky had had an ingenious plan of borrowing a couple of them so *they* could find the tomato worms and save *her* all that trouble. But Brigitte would not let her because of the Café. She said people eating at an outdoor café did not like to see or smell chickens or chicken feathers or chicken poop. It was one of those plans, Lucky realized too late, where you need to just do it instead of asking first, especially when you're pretty sure the answer will be *non*.

"But I do not *want* to cook the hamburger for them," Brigitte was arguing. "At every restaurant and fast food they can eat the hamburger. Here, I say no hamburger. Eat instead something new. I am thinking sometime to put *escargots* on the menu."

"What's that?" Lincoln sounded interested. Unlike Lucky, he loved trying things he'd never tasted before. Plus, he was always, always hungry.

"Oh, Lincoln, they are so delicious baked in their sauce of melted butter and garlic and parsley. When I am little, we go to the countryside after it rains, because it is the time they all come out. We gather many baskets of them, the *petits-gris*, bring them home, and starve them until they become clean inside. One time I remember"—Brigitte broke off and laughed—"one time my papa forget to put a weight on the basket lid. The next morning we find them climbing all over the kitchen."

Lucky listened to the silence inside the trailer, waiting for Lincoln to ask what in the world kind of animal Brigitte was talking about. Horrendous descriptions like this one of Brigitte's always made Lucky a little worried about her adopted mom's parenting skills. Brigitte was only a beginner parent, having been Lucky's guardian for a little over two years. Apparently, it was normal in France, where Brigitte came from, to hunt and starve some poor little creatures before you cooked and ate them.

Finally Lincoln said, "Brigitte, what kind of animals are they?"

"*Escargots*—snails. They are very delicate and beautiful on the plate, and we eat them with the little fork right in their shells." Lucky's squeamishness gland contracted. Gah!

"Come on," Lincoln said. "Why don't the shells break? They'd be too fragile." Lucky could tell that Lincoln didn't for one minute believe this gross, ridiculous story any more than she did.

"*Non*, in France our snails have the very hard shell. I show you the picture in my cookbook." Lucky was tempted to go inside to look at the picture but decided that tomato worms were enough for one day.

Six of them, Lucky counted as she dropped some tomato leaves in the jar and screwed on the lid with its punched holes. She wanted to keep them from starving or suffocating to death before they got eaten by the Captain's chickens. She put the jar in the shade under one of the Café tables. She would take it to the Captain's house after she helped Brigitte prep for tomorrow's lunch.

"Well," she heard Lincoln say as she came inside, "I'm not sure about geologists, but if it's a choice between snails and hamburgers on the menu, I think you're safer with burgers."

Brigitte made a gesture like waving away a fly. "Pfft," she said.

4. paloma

Lucky was not shy at all, being scientifically curious about everything. So on Saturday, when the minivan with a Cal State Northridge decal on its window pulled up, and a pack of geologists sat themselves at the round table of the Café outside, Lucky went straight out from the kitchen trailer with the blackboard menu and a big welcome smile.

Then she saw that one of the geologists was a girl about her own age, who looked a little shy around the edges.

Lucky set the blackboard on its easel and leaned over to the girl—who had on khaki shorts and climbing boots and a camouflage vest and matching hat—Lucky leaned over just like a real waitress and said to her, "Let me know if you have any questions about the menu." The girl was peering at the three connected trailers where Lucky and Brigitte lived: the kitchen trailer in the middle, with Lucky's canned-ham bedroom trailer soldered to one end of it and Brigitte's Westcraft to the other.

And Lucky saw, through the girl's wide-open, amazed-looking eyes, the Café's white-tableclothed tables, the hard-packed sand floor, and the lattice fence to break the wind and give shade. She looked as if she'd never been anyplace like this before, ever.

The girl kind of whispered to Lucky, "Do you get to be the waitress?" like saying with her voice, *How cool is* that?; like wondering if Lucky got to do the best job in the world. So Lucky showed her, yes, by setting up the glasses in a very efficient waitressy way, same as Lulu at Smithy's Family Restaurant in Sierra City, which is a major restaurant open twenty-four hours a day, not just an outdoor place like Brigitte's Hard Pan Café, open for lunch on weekends and holidays only. What you do is you pretend the place setting is a clock, and you put the water glass at exactly one o'clock.

The geologists studied Brigitte's Frenchy handwriting on the menu, and Brigitte came out smiling in her short cotton dress and espadrilles sandals, carrying a pitcher of water on a round tray.

One of the group, a regular customer by the name of Pete, said, "Hey, Brigitte, I brought you some hungry geologists." To the others he said, "Meet Brigitte, the best chef in the Eastern Sierras, and that's her daughter, Lucky." Pete was tall, with big arm muscles and an energetic face. When he spoke, his eyes, eyebrows, mouth, and even his ears moved a great deal; they were acrobatic. Although he was clean shaven, his beard was the type to already be growing out again the minute he finished shaving. It was an enthusiastic beard. Lucky often had an urge to touch his cheeks, which looked scratchy in a handsome way, but instead she stared at them quite hard. When she did this, Pete himself would rub his cheek, as if he were feeling it for her.

He grinned at Brigitte, ears rising up on the sides, and went on, "This is the gang I told you about—been bragging on your food to them, and now we're all doing fieldwork in the area, so I brought them along. This is Sylvia; she's a sedimentologist. Then Dixon—she's the hungry-looking one—mineralogist, and my buddy Erwin the Earthquake Guy, seismologist. Next to him is Rocky—paleontologist—and Rocky's niece, who came along"— he winked at her—"just to worry her mother."

"Well," Brigitte said, "it is good that we have such a lot of rocks around here," which made the geologists laugh. "Do you have any question about the menu today?"

Someone asked whether they served hamburgers. *"Ah, non,"* Brigitte said, looking regretful but at the same time as if this were not the correct question. Then she smiled and explained how the tomatoes were grown organically right there in Hard Pan. "You are going to like them very much," she said, "also the avocado salad today, which has a spicy sauce." Brigitte smiled serenely, to show that they didn't have to worry one bit because all the dishes on the blackboard were delicious.

So everyone ordered cold soups, salads, and iced tea, and Lucky went inside to get a basket of Brigitte's crusty bread and little individually wrapped pats of butter.

There was a tap, and Lucky looked up to see the girl's head poking in. "Is there a bathroom?" she asked.

"Sure," said Lucky, and lifted her chin toward the far end of the trailer. The girl had that way of not looking right at you, which some people think is unfriendly but Lucky understood could also be a certain category of shyness.

So instead of worrying about a possible unfriendly aspect to this girl, Lucky thought of how her tone of voice had said that being the waitress was cool. And that inspired Lucky to make herself look even more professional when the girl re-emerged. Hefting a large tray, she said, "The whole trick to not spilling," as if she were an accomplished waitress training a new one, "is don't look at it. You have to trust your hands and arms to balance everything without supervising them. They know what they're doing."

"Whoa!" the girl said, as she followed Lucky down the

trailer steps and across the hard-packed sand. She said it like she'd never have thought of that tray-carrying tip in a million years.

And then Lucky worried that maybe right now she was being a little bit show-offy, although without really meaning to. "Are you really a geologist?" she asked to change the subject.

The girl shrugged. But then she said, "I might be one when I grow up, which, you get to be outside a lot and wear camo." Lucky peered intently at her eyelashes, which were dark and curly, beautiful little frames for her eyes. There was probably a very good evolutionary reason to have eyelashes like that, and Lucky wondered what that reason would be.

"Hey!" the uncle said to the girl as she sat down, while Lucky distributed plates to each person. "I think you're supposed to keep out of the way, Paloma."

"*Non*, it is okay," said Brigitte. But that name slammed into Lucky like a sonic boom and made her drop her empty tray. Paloma! Paloma was the tragic woman in Miles's story, who got killed when two miners fought over her up at the Lost Brooch Well. And now here was this *other* Paloma, who had *also* come to Hard Pan. It was a zillion-to-one coincidence . . . or it was, Lucky thought, something even more powerful.

As she picked up her tray, brushing off the sand, Lucky realized that she had just seconds ago delivered a little lesson on the correct way to balance one. The girl was watching her, frowning slightly. It could have meant, *Hey, run that by me again, what you said about not spilling*, or it could have just meant, in a good way, *Yikes! What just happened that made you look so surprised?*

Lucky clutched her tray and kept her chin up. She was used to Lincoln, who had never been complicated or mysterious. If only she could decipher whether Paloma was shy but nice versus shy but snobbish. She hoped, strongly, that the verdict would be shy but nice.

"This bread's good," the paleontologist said to the sedimentologist.

"It is to keep your stomachs from getting too wet," Brigitte explained, pouring tea.

Paloma folded her lips inside and cut her eyes sideways at Lucky. This time Lucky was positive that the look was a kind of extra-cool coded way of saying, *Wet stomachs?* Lucky's mouth made a tiny half smile and she cut *her* eyes to the side, meaning, *Don't make me laugh right now!* Then it was time for Lucky to go inside with Brigitte to prepare the lunch plates.

In the kitchen trailer, Brigitte seemed to have five arms, and all of them were moving at once. Lucky had noticed that when the Café was full of customers and Brigitte was cooking or serving, she kind of speeded up, like a sled going downhill. She hummed her French tunes and seemed to become somehow lighter, as if she could move around without having to use her legs. Whipping the salad dressing, grating carrots, and ladling soup into bowls, Brigitte said, "What are you and that girl saying together? She is nice, yes? Her name means—what is the name of the bird that came to the ark of Noah after the flood?"

Lucky nodded. "Dove," she said as she cranked the handle of the parsley grinder over the finger-sized slices of avocado. "We didn't really talk much, but I think I like her."

And Lucky believed that, because of her name, and also having a geologist uncle who was a friend of Pete's, Paloma had been *destined* to come to Hard Pan. But what Lucky liked about the name especially, and hoped would be a sort of prediction, was the very first part of it: a syllable that could stand by itself, a separate word embedded in her name. Lucky also had a whole separate word in her own name, so they had that amazing coincidence of first syllables already in common.

They had pal and luck. At least, Lucky hoped so.

5. tomorrow's specialty

The geologists and Paloma seemed to be enjoying their meal. Lucky watched out the window to be ready, when they were finished, to clear the plates. Suddenly she saw Paloma lean over and look beneath the table.

Lucky remembered her jar of tomato worms from yesterday, and a bad feeling coated her stomach.

Paloma's head stayed down for a few minutes. Then it came up again, and in her hand was the glass jar. Lucky glanced at Brigitte, who had her back turned, stacking plates. In a flash, Lucky was out the trailer and down the steps, but not in time to keep Paloma from saying, "'Luscious tomatoes'? Which, it looks more like avocado pieces with a bunch of leaves."

"It *is* avocado," said Lucky. "Slices of avocado in a kind of . . . dressing. Special French dressing with leaves." She reached for the jar, but the sedimentologist beat her to it.

Leaning in and trying to peer around the jar's label, the

seismologist said, "That dressing was really wonderful. Kind of mustardy." He squinted. "My glasses are in the car, so I can't—"

The sedimentologist held the jar up, trying to get a view through the bottom. She said, "But why are the avocado slices kept outside in a jar under the table?"

"Let me see that," said the mineralogist. The trouble with geologists is they all want to examine everything.

"You know, these things aren't avocado slices. They're some kind of *creatures*," the mineralogist said. "They're *moving*."

Paloma's uncle snatched the jar. "They're worms," he said. "Tomato worms. That's what I thought right away, but then I thought, *nah*. Why would they have a jar of tomato worms under the table of a restaurant?"

24 Lucky glanced at the trailer and saw the back of Brigitte's head through the window. Safe so far, but she had to get rid of that jar fast. "Okay, you're right, they're tomato worms. We're fattening them up so Brigitte can . . ." Creative juices sprayed the inside of Lucky's brain, like water spurting out of a sprinkler that had been clogged. She remembered the gross story of the snails.

Lucky looked all the geologists in the eye and said, "So Brigitte can cook them. They will be the specialty on the menu tomorrow."

"No kidding!" Pete said, and his face leaped to attention. "I never heard of tomato worms being edible. You mean like *escargots*?"

Lucky noticed that Paloma had tucked her lips in again, and she stared at Lucky with wide eyes.

"Exactly right," said Lucky. "They're a lot like snails, but without the shells. In France they are very"—she searched for a word that would make her sound like she knew what she was talking about—"very . . . *prized*." She smiled confidently in the way of someone who has pointed out a clear, obvious fact. "So I better take these guys in now so we can starve them until they're clean inside." She grabbed the jar and ran for her own trailer, flung the door open, tossed the jar on her bed, and ran back out.

Brigitte came out with her tray. Paloma and all the geologists turned to her with their eyebrows up.

A lot of worry churned around in Lucky's corpuscles. She knew Brigitte would not like the tomato-worm episode one bit. Telling customers strange stories about tomorrow's menu was *not* something recommended in the online Certified Course in Restaurant Management and Administration with Diploma from the Culinary Institute of France in Paris. "I was just telling about tomorrow's special," Lucky said, "because—"

"Because everyone loved their avocado salads a *lot*," Paloma interrupted, "and we were talking about the dressing."

The sedimentologist frowned at Paloma and said, "Well, what actually happened—"

"Was that we were all thinking," Pete interrupted, talking to Brigitte but smiling in a piercing, squinty-eyed way at the sedimentologist and speaking each word very deliberately, "about how *nice* and *refreshing* it is when fruits and vegetables don't have sprays or chemicals on them. It's perfectly *natural* to get a bug or a worm or two on them once in a while, right?"

Brigitte's spine got straighter and her eyes blazed. "Someone has found the bug in the avocado salad?" she asked. "Where is this bug?"

"Oh, no," Paloma put in quickly. "Which, it wasn't in the food—just under the table."

Lucky smiled her eyes at Paloma in thanks. At the same time, she tried to make herself as unnoticeable to Brigitte as a tomato worm on a tomato branch, or even a caterpillar disguised as a bird dropping, and she wished someone would change the subject. She sent powerful brain waves of *dessert, dessert, dessert, dessert, dessert* to the mineralogist, paleontologist, sedimentologist, and seismologist.

"Dixon," Pete said to the mineralogist, who was frowning at the door of the canned-ham trailer, "on the drive up from L.A., weren't you talking about that time you had a great dessert when you were in Paris?"

Lucky's powerful brain waves had worked! Brigitte's spine relaxed a little, and she said, "You will like the fresh pears poached in red wine, a *spécialité* from the south of France."

Everybody ordered the pears, and they finally seemed to have forgotten the jar of worms. But when Lucky got busy clearing the table, she caught Paloma looking back at her as if she could barely keep from bursting out laughing. It was a private, sparky glint of a glance. That secret eye-code launched a little YouTube video in Lucky's brain, of herself showing Paloma one of her favorite places in Hard Pan: the broken-down cart behind Dot's Baubles 'n' Beauty Salon. In Lucky's imagined video, she and Paloma scrunched down in the cart, and watched and listened as people got their hair done on Dot's back porch and told Dot stuff that usually you only tell your doctor. At the end, a bunch of Hard Pan ladies, all with the exact same bluish, tight-curled hairdo, which was Dot's specialty, admired themselves in little mirrors while Lucky and Paloma clamped their hands over their mouths to keep the laughter from spurting out. This is the kind of picture Lucky got in her mind to go with the words "best friend."

27

It made Lucky realize that no one had ever given her that exact kind of look before. She concluded, a little sadly, that although she and Lincoln had gone through their whole childhoods together, he was just too serious and, well, *predictable*. Anyone who ever met Lincoln knew that, eventually, he would learn how to tie every knot in the world and he would understand the uses for those knots. He was not the kind of person who would get in trouble just for the fun of it, or for the sake of an adventure, or to find out how intrepid he could be. Now that Paloma had shared such a secret, private look—almost like an invitation—a certain insight came to Lucky about Lincoln. He was reliable, calm, orderly, and, on top of that, a boy. A boy who was going to leave the whole country. It wasn't entirely his fault. But standing as she was on the tip of the mountain of ten, about to transform her 11 into a pair of skis and fly off in a blur of speed, what Lucky wanted was a *girl* best friend, an adventurous girl. And without even knowing that she'd been looking, now Lucky longed for that girl to be Paloma.

6. learn to swim at home

Looking out the window over her sink full of sudsy water, Lucky could see Paloma and the geologists eating their dessert. She didn't mind washing dishes and was good at it. Her hands liked wearing rubber gloves because they could plunge into really hot scalding soapy water and not care one bit. But then through the window she saw Paloma sad-eyebrowing her and making a funny wiggling gesture with her index finger. Suddenly Lucky got that it meant *Poor worms!* And she nodded and shrugged and blew out her cheeks to mean, *Yeah, poor worms; wish I didn't have to be in here doing these dishes!* And right then she wondered if maybe she should invite Paloma for a visit in her bedroom trailer.

Trying to see the trailer through Paloma's eyes, Lucky had to admit that it was not at all like a regular, normal girl's bedroom: The varnish was chipping off the old curved wood walls, there was dog hair on the little rug, and you couldn't fit much more than Lucky, her dog HMS Beagle, and one other person inside. The smallness of it didn't bother Lucky; in fact, it gave evidence of an eerie and wonderful connection to the scientist Charles Darwin. Lucky's trailer and Darwin's cabin in *HMS Beagle* were almost exactly the same size. Because of this and several other miraculous coincidences, it was clear to Lucky that her destiny was connected to Charles Darwin's. In her mind was a list of the similarities:

Lucky Trimble
Dedicated scientist from childhood
Notices how animals adapt to their habitat
Sleeps in trailer size of cabin in HMS Beagle
Collects insect specimens
Dog's name is HMS Beagle
Mother died when she was eight

Charles Darwin
Dedicated scientist from childhood
Noticed how animals adapt to their habitat
Slept in ship cabin same size as canned-ham trailer
Collected insect specimens
Ship's name was HMS Beagle
Mother died when he was eight

The part about HMS Beagle wasn't a coincidence; Lucky named her dog for the ship because *it*, the ship, had been named for a dog, but still it was another link between her world and his.

But what if Paloma didn't like the canned-ham trailer? Being used to Lincoln, Lucky wasn't sure how it worked to be friends with girls. Did you have to tell *every* secret? Were you supposed to show you were cool by using swear words? No, Paloma was definitely a fun type of person, not a bad-mouth type. Lucky's optimism gland started pumping and she felt that kind of excitement of right before you open a present. She finished rinsing plates and said, "Brigitte, can I invite Paloma to see my trailer? I could finish washing later."

Brigitte smiled and frowned at the same time, her mouth twisting down and then up at the corners. Lucky had never seen anyone else do this, so she figured it was a handy thing French people developed, in order for their faces to show that you can have good thoughts and bad thoughts on the same subject at the same time.

"It would be so sad," Lucky pressed on in a small, tragic voice, "for me to miss the only chance in my whole life to have a real best friend."

Brigitte laughed. "Lucky," she said, "you are so dramatic. What about Lincoln? Always I think he is your best friend."

"He's my friend, but he's a *boy*. You can't be best friends with a boy."

"*Ah, bon?*" Brigitte said, which Lucky figured meant, *Are you sure about that?* Then she grinned and said, "Yes, go and ask her inside while the others finish to eat their pears."

Lucky bounded out to the tables.

"Want to see my canned ham?" she asked Paloma, which made the geologists look at her with surprised little smiles.

"Sure!" Paloma said, and jumped up. Lucky led the way.

"Where is it?" Paloma asked once they were in Lucky's bedroom trailer.

"You're in it."

Paloma looked around at the curved wood ceiling and at the porthole windows and burst out laughing. "Now I get it! It's the shape!" she said. "I thought—well, I thought you meant an actual canned *ham*! Which, this bedroom is so totally original! You have your own personal trailer, like a movie star on a *set*."

Lucky now saw her trailer in a new way. It was actually cool.

32   Paloma plopped down on the bed. "So how'd you get a French mom?"

Lucky picked up the jar of tomato worms and plopped next to her. "Adopted."

"You *adopted* her?"

This sounded way cooler than *being* adopted, and, Lucky told herself, she *had* kind of adopted Brigitte.

"Yeah. It's kind of complicated and they're still doing the paperwork, but Brigitte got her green card, so yeah."

"Wow." Paloma bounced a little bit on the bed. "So why do you really have that jar of worms?"

"Oh, I just hunted these off the tomato plants. They're kind of a gift."

Paloma burst out laughing again.

"What?" asked Lucky, a little concerned that Paloma was laughing at her.

"Um, a gift? Tomato worms?"

"For some chickens I know," Lucky explained.

"I can't decide which is weirder—tomato worms on tomorrow's menu or giving tomato worms as a *present* to some *chickens*." Lucky could see how it looked weird to Paloma, but cool-weird, not dumb-weird.

In a formal, professor-y voice, Paloma said, "My dear mineralogist, would you please pass that salad of highly prized worms, which, it has such a delicious French dressing." She pretend-smoothed her shiny black hair, tilting up her chin.

Lucky wiped her lips with an imaginary napkin and held out the LUSCIOUS TOMATOES jar, with her little finger elegantly lifted as if she were a queen holding a teacup. "Certainly, my dear sedimentologist," she said in a fake British-queen accent. "I was saving a few as a gift for some chickens I know, but I'd rather you have them. Chickens are so thoughtless about gifts, anyway."

"How sad and how true," Paloma murmured. She was pretty in a unique way, with a round mouth full of lots and lots of nicely even teeth. Her eyelashes, of course, were gorgeous, but her dark blue eyes drooped a little at the edges. If you put eyes like that on some other person, all you'd really notice would be their droopiness. But on Paloma's face they made you suddenly wonder if eye shadow would make your own eyes look more like hers.

And, especially, you wanted to make Paloma laugh. Getting her to smile was easy because her mouth was the opposite of ordinary mouths, in that usually lips are relaxed when they're closed and not doing anything. With Paloma, her lips were at *rest* when she was smiling; otherwise she had to sort of unsmile. It was practically the best and most interesting face Lucky had ever seen.

"What's that an ad for?" Paloma asked, looking at a clipping from the back of a magazine that Lucky had tacked on her wall.

"Swimming lessons," said Lucky.

"*Swimming* lessons?" Paloma got off the bed and went to study the advertisement. It was a picture of a short-haired boy, about their age, sitting on a stool in front of a table. On the table was a big clear plastic bucket-sized container full of water, and the boy was leaning over it with his head turned to the side, one ear pointed down at the water. He wasn't wearing a shirt, and his arms were windmilling around in the air like a swimmer doing the crawl stroke. At the bottom of the picture were the words,

LEARN TO SWIM AT HOME. ONLY $39.95 FOR 6 LESSONS.

Paloma frowned at the ad, glanced at Lucky, looked back at the ad, and burst out laughing.

Lucky positioned a pretend bucket of water on a pretend table in front of her. She stuck her face down into the pretend water and made her arms flail all around. "Help, I'm drowning!" she said.

Paloma said in a stern voice, "You should have studied your lessons more carefully! You know you're not supposed to go into the deep end yet!"

Lucky laughed so hard she made a loud bubble-popping snorkle noise in her throat, which caused Paloma to shriek. Tears ran down their faces.

"Thirty-nine dollars and ninety-five cents!" said Lucky, and collapsed onto the bed, clutching her stomach.

"Six lessons!" said Paloma, and pressed the edge of her T-shirt against her eyes. "But does that include"—her voice got higher as she squeezed out her words while at the same time being convulsed with laughter—"does that include the back-stroke?"

HMS Beagle wandered in from the kitchen and went politely over to smell Paloma.

Paloma held out her palm for the Beag to sniff. She gulped down deep breaths and got herself to stop laughing. "Hi, girl," she said, and stroked one of the silky golden ears. "Wow, she's big. What's her name?"

"HMS Beagle."

"HMS Beagle?" Paloma made her face very serious. She put her hand on Lucky's shoulder. "I have to tell you something, Lucky," she said. "Which, brace yourself. That dog is not a beagle." Lucky could see that Paloma was working hard to hold in her smile.

"I know," Lucky said in the same serious voice. "She's named for Charles Darwin's ship."

Paloma couldn't hold it any longer. She collapsed into herself on the bed, snorting and choking and holding her stomach. Lucky hadn't meant for naming HMS Beagle to be funny, but now she saw that it was, unbearably. It had been transformed into *unbearable* funniness. Her bones melted and couldn't hold her up anymore. She rolled onto the floor.

HMS Beagle wrinkled her forehead and looked at Lucky, who was gasping and crying and trying to explain about Charles Darwin. Lucky looked back at her dog, pointed, and spewed laughter into her hands. Paloma did the same, while HMS Beagle padded out toward the kitchen, her head low. This made Lucky and Paloma burst out in a new wave of laughing.

Lucky discovered that hard laughing was like crying in the sense that sometimes you cannot stop. And it's a catching disease, because when another person is spurting and gasping it makes you start again even after you have taken deep gulps of air and stopped looking at the other laughing person. The laughter muscles in your stomach ache because they're not used to it. Lucky calmed herself and cleared her throat and wiped her eyes on her sleeve.

Lucky loved having to laugh so hard that she couldn't stop, and she loved teetering on the tightrope of keeping much,

much more laughter inside, and she loved making Paloma get hysterical. But now her face and her torso were achy from laughing, and she felt wrung out. She could see that it was the same for Paloma. They both sagged onto the bed.

Suddenly they heard a tugboat outside the trailer, coming closer and closer. Lucky blotted her eyes with her shirt and blew her nose into a paper towel.

"Lucky," Paloma said, making her voice very calm and low.

"Yes, Paloma," Lucky said in the same controlled, TV-broadcaster voice.

"I believe there is a tugboat coming this way, although I didn't notice any ocean in the area."

So just when they thought they were laughed out, exhausted, and completely dried up, wanting something else like a Gatorade and a Pixy Stix, they were off again. Their humor ducts opened up and spewed laughter into their bodies.

When Miles knocked and then came into Lucky's trailer, he stared at them for a while, boneless and writhing and hiccuping and gasping. Then he made more tugboat noises until they begged him to stop, and flung themselves outside, screaming with the craziness and strangeness of Miles and HMS Beagle and weird magazine ads and tomato worms, their arms looped around each other's shoulders, smiled on by Brigitte and the pack of geologists, matching their steps without even meaning to.

7. a plan

Uncle Rocky and the geologists had promised to stop by for coffee and brownies the next day, Sunday afternoon, before the long drive back to the San Fernando Valley. Early that morning Paloma called Lucky from the hotel in Sierra City.

"So how did they like their gift?" Paloma said.

Lucky thought she'd missed something in the conversation. "Who?"

"The chickens!"

Lucky laughed and said in her fake British-queen accent, "Oh, superb, you know, especially with the garlic and butter sauce." In her regular voice she added, "I wish you could come back next weekend."

"Me too. I wish Hard Pan wasn't so far. It's like two hundred miles."

"Yeah, but the geologists love it here. Maybe your uncle will come back and bring you."

"We need a plan," said Paloma. "Let's each try to think of one and compare notes when I get there."

When the minivan stuffed with geologists and Paloma arrived that afternoon, Lucky was still working hard on a plan for the next weekend. It would be one of the last with balmy, warm nights, and Brigitte had talked about a little celebration for Lucky's birthday.

Through her porthole window, Lucky watched everyone climb out of the minivan. Pete and Uncle Rocky set up a laptop at one of the Café tables and hunched over it, talking excitedly and peering together at the screen. The seismologist, sedimentologist, and mineralogist stood around stretching and drinking from their water bottles.

Carrying a tray outside, Lucky scrunched up one side of her mouth as a way of showing Paloma that she didn't have an actual plan yet but was working on it. Paloma nodded at the brownies as an answer that at least everyone would be in a good brownie-eating mood. They could tell what each other was thinking, as if their brains had a wireless connection.

"Check out these rock layers—beautiful data from right up on the hill," Pete said to Brigitte, showing her the photograph on his laptop screen. "We're going to look further next weekend, on our own time, just for fun, if Rocky can get away. We figure if we leave L.A. on Friday afternoon, we'll have two good days to poke around and, most important, two Hard Pan Café meals." Lucky and Paloma stared at each other with wide eyes and flopped into chairs. Lucky eyebrowed Paloma as code for *This is going smoothly without our even having made a plan yet!*

Brigitte peered at the screen. "These layers of rocks are making me think of a *croque-monsieur*," she said, meaning a sandwich with layers of ham and cheese. "Maybe I will make them for lunch next Saturday or Sunday."

Pete's eyes opened wide and his eyebrows jumped up. "Then I'll be coming for sure, even if Rocky can't," he said. Lucky's anxiety glands contracted. What if Paloma's uncle Rocky couldn't get away?

"If they come, can Paloma come too and sleep over?" Lucky asked, aiming her question at Brigitte but hoping Paloma's uncle would understand she was also asking him. "She's already famous in Hard Pan—there's an old legend about a beautiful woman named Paloma, and a piece of jewelry in the Found Object Wind Chime Museum and Visitor Center that Paloma has to come back and see because it was a gift to her namesake." Lucky had told Paloma the legend with all its gory details, but she didn't go into those now. She didn't want to alarm Uncle Rocky or have him talk about murder to Paloma's parents.

"Please?" Paloma added. "It would be really educational and cultural, going to the museum."

Rocky shrugged and smiled at his niece. "It's okay with me if your folks don't mind. But your mother is a little concerned about supervision." To Brigitte, Uncle Rocky explained, "Paloma's mom thinks it's the Wild West out here and got worked up about snakes and scorpions and sunstroke and who knows what-all.

Dehydration. Paloma getting lost in the desert. Hantavirus. Wild burros. You name it." He shook his head to show that *he* didn't agree that all those bad things would happen. "She still thinks of me as her little kid brother who doesn't take things seriously. I had to promise not to let Paloma out of my sight—don't know if my sister will agree to a sleepover."

"Well, it is not really so wild in Hard Pan," said Brigitte. Lucky had noticed that Brigitte's back always got a little bit straighter when people said anything critical about Hard Pan. "Lucky and I are very happy to have Paloma as our guest. I call her mother to make the invitation if you give me her telephone number. I will explain that there was only that one time that I find the snake in the clothes dryer."

All the geologists laughed, but Lucky did not find this funny. "Brigitte, please leave out the part about the snake," she said. To Rocky she added, "It was only a red racer. And I promise we won't get lost in the desert like I almost did the time I was trying to run away, and we'll wear lots of sunscreen and"—Lucky searched for more ways to reassure Uncle Rocky about Paloma's safety—"and you can tell Paloma's mom that all the tarantulas are finished crossing the road by now because I haven't seen any in about a week."

"Oh, well, then," Uncle Rocky said in a serious voice that meant, Lucky knew, that he was teasing her. "Sounds like that about covers all the possible dangers." Lucky understood that Paloma's uncle's teasing wasn't *mean* teasing, but she wished he understood how very, very serious the subject was, about Paloma coming back next weekend. Rocky must have read the look on Lucky's face, because he said, "Don't worry; I'll do my best." Paloma jumped up and went behind Rocky's seat to hug him from behind, then did a little dance over to Brigitte and hugged her in a quick, shy way. Lucky saw Uncle Rocky jam his cap on his head to hide his ears, which had become red exactly as Lincoln's did when he was embarrassed, and Lucky exchanged a secret triumphant look with Paloma.

42   Sometimes certain things are so important, so vital and urgent, that they get a momentum of their own, like a force of nature. Lucky felt sure that the essentialness of Paloma coming back to Hard Pan was exactly that kind of force of nature, and one way or another, it would happen.

8. short sammy's box

On Monday morning, as Lucky and HMS Beagle waited with Miles and Lincoln for the school bus, a noisy white pickup crested the hill and cruised down into Hard Pan, braking at the

SLOW:
CHILDREN
AT
PLAY

sign. Most everyone, people and dogs, when they heard a vehicle arriving, would turn to see who it was and where it was going. HMS Beagle knew certain vehicles by sound, and by watching her dog, Lucky got a heads-up on whether or not something exciting or interesting might be about to happen.

They saw two men in the pickup's cab and a huge rectangular wooden crate in the bed. None of them knew the vehicle, and they hoped it would get to its destination before the bus arrived so they'd have a chance to figure out what was going on. HMS Beagle stood fully alert, ears forward, black nose twitching.

When it pulled up near Short Sammy's water tank house, Lucky was sure that each and every Hard Panner's curiosity glands were pumping overtime. Short Sammy didn't get too many visitors from out of town, and it would be interesting to know, if that big wooden box was being delivered to him, what was in it. He didn't have a lot of stuff, and he didn't *want* a lot of stuff. There was his guitar, his radio for listening to the traffic reports from Los Angeles, and his big black cast-iron frying pan. Short Sammy's only other great treasure had been his dog, Roy.

Lucky knew, from the way Short Sammy sometimes glanced at the photo of his dog in its sardine-can frame, that he missed Roy; he missed him a lot.

The dog had survived a bite on his scrotum by a rattlesnake in the days before Short Sammy quit drinking. Sammy's wife had left him right after that incident, and she had taken Roy with her. But whatever the pickup truck was bringing, it surely wasn't the one thing Short Sammy wanted—Roy.

Lucky noticed the Captain peering out from his observation tower, a three-foot-square glass-sided enclosure that stuck up from his roof like a see-through chimney. The Captain liked to keep tabs on goings-on around town. Dot and Mrs. Prender had come out of their houses, both apparently finding that they had important things to take care of outdoors, and they (like Lucky, Miles, Lincoln, and HMS Beagle) watched the truck as it slowed at the post with Short Sammy's address on it.

Nine dented and rusty enamel tea-kettles were bolted to the post, which made it interesting and noticeable. Short Sammy had painted

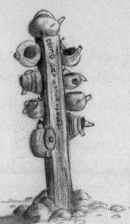

230 Dry Gulch Street

in red letters that began at the top and went down. No one else bothered with posts or street signs or addresses, because it was just as easy to give your visitor directions like, "Turn left at the 'Slow: Children at Play' sign" or "Go just past the cabin with four washing machines in the front yard," and all the mail came to P.O. boxes at the post office. But Short Sammy said he liked having an actual address and wanted it to be visible on his teakettle post.

45

The driver pulled up and parked beside Sammy's house, and all the Hard Panners who were busy with weeding and rak-ing and rug shaking, plus the Captain in his observation tower and those waiting for the school bus, watched. The driver and the passenger, who wore T-shirts, jeans, and baseball caps, stood talking with Sammy a moment, and then they all grouped around the truck bed, leaning on their elbows to look in.

"They're figuring out how to move the box," Lincoln said. "Bet it's heavy."

Sammy gestured and pointed, and the driver jerked down the tailgate, which made a loud rusty shriek. The three men lifted out a flat wheeled cart and set it on the ground. Then they carefully angled and slid out the very large and heavy wooden box, positioned it on the cart, and rolled it to a spot at the side of Sammy's front door. They heaved it off the cart and onto the ground.

After the truck left, instead of sitting outside on a lawn chair in the shade, where neighbors could stroll by and comment about the box in order to get him to tell them what was in it, Short Sammy went inside and pulled his door shut. Everyone knew this meant that he didn't want visitors.

"What's in Short Sammy's box?" Miles asked.

Lucky thought about it. "No idea," she said.

"I don't like it," Lincoln said. "It's exactly the size and shape of a—" He stopped.

"Of a what?" Miles asked.

Lincoln looked at Miles and frowned. He said, "I think the bus is coming," and as Miles turned to look, Lincoln gave Lucky a silent message, a tiny, quick shake of the head while flicking his eyes toward Miles. Lucky understood: He didn't want to say whatever it was in Miles's hearing. She nodded, agreeing not to discuss it then.

Miles was the first to board, greeting Sandi the bus driver enthusiastically. "Short Sammy got a big box delivered to him just now," he told her.

"Back of the bus," Sandi said, as she always did, checking her side-view mirror.

A moment later Lincoln boarded and walked backward

slowly down the long aisle to the very end of the bus, talking to Lucky in a low voice. "I hate to even say it. It's very sad," he said.

Lucky hadn't found anything sad about the big wooden box. "Why sad?" she asked.

"Lucky, when you look at the size and shape of that box and how heavy it was, there's only one thing it can be!"

"Well, what?" Lucky said.

Lincoln stopped walking and leaned toward her, whispering. "The only thing it can be is a . . . No, it doesn't make sense."

"Hurry up and take your seats!" Sandi yelled.

"Lincoln! What?"

"No, I'm sure I'm wrong. Let's forget it. Short Sammy will tell us if he wants us to know." Lincoln swung into the nearest seat, moving over to the window. Lucky kept walking, touching the seat backs on either side of the aisle for balance. She'd suddenly realized what Lincoln had been thinking. He'd concluded that the box was a casket.

She felt her heart beating as if it were trying to escape from her chest.

Short Sammy was going to die.

9. s'mores

Some of the things Brigitte tried and practiced and wished for, in her goal of getting her American citizenship and becoming a "real" Californian, seemed strange to Lucky. But Brigitte's efforts and struggles made Lucky (and a lot of other people in Hard Pan) realize that, just by being born here, they were experts on California-ness and American-ness. And advising Brigitte could be pretty fun. Her campaign got a lot of momentum when she bought a Weber barbecue at the Sierra City Thrift Store. She'd cleaned it and polished it and listened when Lincoln advised her never to use scavenged wood for making charcoal, because it could have chemicals like anti-termite poison in it. To Brigitte, a Weber in her yard—where everyone could see it—was solid proof of her California-ness.

Brigitte had invited Lincoln, Miles and his grandmother Mrs. Prender, Short Sammy, and Dot for dinner on Monday to celebrate the first meal cooked on her good-as-new Weber.

Everyone, adults and kids, knew not to talk to Sammy about his box. Even Miles, now that he was nearly six, understood about *minding your own business*. At the same time, Lucky worried and worried. She hoped that Sammy would bring up the subject of his box himself and explain that it wasn't a casket at all.

Dinner was ribs and corn on the cob served on paper plates, with lemonade to drink.

"This is a *very* typical American-Californian dinner," Lucky said, as a way to make Brigitte consider cooking it often.

Miles showed Brigitte how to roll her corncob directly on the stick of butter, turning and turning until it was glistening and the stick of butter had a little dip of a saddle in the center.

"We do not eat corn in this way in France," Brigitte said. "While it is still attached to its cob. Are you sure it is polite to put your corn right on the stick of butter?"

"Oh, for sure," said Lucky, who loved corn on the cob and felt sad for French people not eating it. In a delicate, artistic way, she scraped the kernels off her cob to create a certain pattern, using her front teeth to eat around two somewhat crooked lines of bright yellow corn. When she was done, a wobbly number eleven stood out against the white cob. Then she ate those kernels too, wishing that turning eleven would make it easier to figure out things like mysterious big heavy boxes.

Lucky had not told Brigitte her worries about Sammy's box being a casket. He acted normal, not like someone who was getting ready to die, but Lucky wasn't sure. She kept her worries inside herself, because talking about them, she believed, would make something bad happen.

After dinner they stayed around the Weber, lounging on the old Chevy and Ford truck seats that had been salvaged from the dump. The seats, neatly mended with duct tape so their insides wouldn't smush out, were grouped by the barbecue in a side area apart from the outdoor tables of the Café.

"Now for the surprise," said Miles. "A very typical American *dessert*." The sun had dipped behind the Coso Mountains, and light was beginning to seep out of the sky. But Miles's face shone as if excitement came in a little tube and it had been rubbed all over him.

"Ice cream?" Brigitte guessed.

"Even more American," Miles said.

"Brownies?"

"Even *more* American." Lucky could tell that Miles loved having important information in his brain that wasn't known by an adult. He had become an authority on typical American food and how to eat it. "And it's a dessert we're going to cook on the Weber!"

Brigitte looked intrigued. "Tell me!" she said.

Bouncing on the seat, Miles cried, "S'mores!" He ran to Mrs. Prender's VW for the ingredients as Lincoln added a few more coals to the barbecue.

Brigitte had never heard of s'mores before, so Miles put himself in charge of teaching her the finer points of making them.

"First, each person has to cook their marshmallow," he said in a teacherish voice, distributing metal skewers to everyone. "Not until it's burned, just try to get it melty and brown." Miles stood at the Weber, demonstrating his technique of turning constantly to achieve even brownness. "But if you get it too cooked, it's okay, because the inside will still be good. Then you quick smear it onto the cookie part"—carefully he slid the marshmallow onto a graham cracker, dropped the skewer on the ground, and licked his fingers—"and plop the chocolate on"—Lucky handed him a small square of Hershey bar—"while it's still hot so the marshmallow melts it, and another graham cracker on top. But you have to be very careful or you'll burn your fingers for sure." Miles took his eyes off this project (it required quite a lot of concentration in order to keep any of the ingredients from falling off) to see if Brigitte was paying attention.

"Okay," she said seriously, poking a marshmallow onto her own skewer, "now I do one."

Miles blew on his little sandwichy dessert, took a small bite, and said to Brigitte, "Bet you don't know why they're called s'mores."

Brigitte turned her marshmallow carefully. "I think it is named for a certain region of America," she said, "which is famous for its desserts."

Lucky laughed. "No," she said, "it's—"

"Wait! Don't tell her!" Miles shouted. "Guess again, Brigitte! *S'mores*!" He pronounced the word exaggeratedly, as a hint.

"It's named for Captain Smor," Lincoln said, "who was known for fighting duels with barbecue skewers."

Miles glared at Lincoln, saw that he was teasing, and rapped his skewer against the Weber. "Lincoln, be serious. I'm *trying* to help Brigitte get more American! She really needs to know stuff like about s'mores."

"Okay," Lincoln said. "You're right. Go ahead and tell her the real truth."

Miles shouted, "Because you always want s'more!"

Brigitte frowned. She didn't get it. This, to Lucky, was a perfect example of why it was so hard for Brigitte to learn how to become more American. It was because of the way that Brigitte thought like a French person, in a logical, orderly way. In Lucky's opinion, when it came to something like s'mores, you had to be able to think in a way that was a little bit silly.

Miles explained, "Because you want *some more*. S'more! Now do you get it?"

"Ah!" Brigitte said, and she laughed, her eyes reflecting the light from the Weber's low flames. "Of course, now I do," she said. "You are right to teach me this amusing name, Miles, and I am glad to have such a clever teacher for becoming more American."

"They tested him out at the school," Mrs. Prender shouted. "Said his IQ is genius level." Lucky wasn't surprised. Miles had told her about the testing, which he'd actually enjoyed. Now that Miles knew how to read, he suddenly seemed to be able to read anything. He loved the Henry and Mudge series, but he also read much harder books. His recent favorite was a book called *Brain Surgery for Beginners*.

"*Plus*, I'm turning six next Sunday," Miles said, as if being a genius and having a birthday at the same time were a special, lifetime achievement. "And the day after that is Lucky's birthday, and she'll be eleven. I wish we could have a big party."

Lucky smiled. She knew that Brigitte had already started making plans for a combined party.

"Big, like how big?" Lincoln said.

Lucky shrugged. "Oh, all of us plus your parents," she said.

"No," Miles said. "It should be everyone! A great big enormous party! We should invite the whole entire town of Hard Pan!"

10. big, big wishes

"You know we can't, Miles," Mrs. Prender bellowed. "We talked already. I can't do with a lot of people at my place. It's too small, and I can't afford it anyway."

"But I'm *finally* turning *six*!" Miles explained patiently, as if his grandmother just wasn't getting the point. "If you add us up, Lucky and I are turning *seventeen*!"

Lucky wondered what kind of celebration most eleven-year-old birthday girls would want, and decided probably not a combined party with a cute, very stubborn, genius-IQ six-year-old. Suddenly she saw herself in a fancy ski lodge at Mammoth Lakes with high ceilings and candles. She was wearing her hair in a gorgeous swept-back way so it didn't have its usual garden hedge look, with a headband made of glittery rhinestones, and a blue-sequined dress, and shiny matching blue eye shadow. She saw herself in the fancy hotel's marble bathroom with her guest, Paloma, who would have a mascara wand in her purse that she would show Lucky how to use. And Lucky would confess to her about staring at Pete-the-geologist's scratchy cheeks and wanting to touch them.

Lucky knew the problem with her ideal birthday dream: It would be too expensive, way too expensive.

Brigitte said, "Yes, Miles, and you will love this party, another very Californian barbecue like tonight, and for dessert there will be some more some-mores." No one corrected her. They all knew she'd need plenty of coaching to learn to say s'mores the right way.

After a while Miles nodded. He seemed to accept the situation of a small birthday party instead of a big celebration with the whole town. He stood at the Weber, mechanically turning his skewer, his head bowed,

 his back to the group. Lucky noticed that the marshmallow was finished cooking, but Miles just stood there, turning and turning.

"No, man," Short Sammy said suddenly. "Let's have the party up at my place. I only got three chairs, but there's room for everyone in the town and then some."

Brigitte looked doubtful, and Mrs. Prender shook her head. Mrs. Prender seemed to be speaking for both of them when she said, "Nice a you to offer, but I still can't afford no food and what-not for forty-three people, even with Brigitte and me sharing the costs."

Short Sammy adjusted his cowboy hat and stretched his legs in their pointy-toed boots. "Naw. I mean I'll *host* the party. I'll cook up a big stew."

Miles's marshmallow caught fire, but he didn't notice. He turned it, unseeing, and waited.

"That house of yours would need festivating," said Dot. "It looks like a water tank."

"Well, it *is* a water tank," Short Sammy said.

"It's a water tank with a great big box by the front door," Dot said darkly. Lucky held her breath, wondering what would happen now that the whole situation had been brought out in the open. Dot plowed on. "That box gonna stay there, or what?" she demanded.

"Nope," Sammy said. "Gonna take what's in the box out of the box, man. Then I'll sink that thing in the ground about halfway. It'll be a surprise. And that's all I'm saying about it right now." He crossed his arms in front of his chest and pulled his cowboy hat down over his eyes. Everyone knew you couldn't get Sammy to say another word when he did that. It was like a CLOSED sign in a store window.

"But Sammy," Lucky said, "can't you tell us at least if it's a good surprise or a bad surprise?"

Sammy tilted his head back, looking at Lucky from under

the brim. "I imagine for some folks it'll be a shocker and cause a lot of fuss; for others, maybe, pretty funny; and someone else'll probably like the idea so much they'll steal it from me. But I don't want the whole town talking about it, deciding if it's good or bad, until I'm ready. And that, man, will be the day of the party."

There was a long silence. Lucky thought and thought about what Sammy had said, trying to figure out what he meant. If it was a casket, why bury it only halfway? That would just be too weird. Lucky looked around, but everyone was staring down at the ground, as if they were trying to understand too, or as if they were praying.

Finally Lincoln cleared his throat. "I'll help you decorate, Dot," he said. "I'm good at climbing ladders. You can tell me what to do. We'll get the Captain to haul folding chairs up from the museum so people can sit out front in the yard."

"Seems like a lot of fuss—," Mrs. Prender began.

Brigitte said, "Next weekend we are busy at the Café with quite a few lunch reservations. Can we have this birthday for Miles and Lucky in the evening on Sunday? I will help you with the food, Sammy, and I will make a big cake because it is too many people each to make their own some-mores."

"Good by me, man," Sammy said, pushing his hat back off his forehead. "But I got the stew covered. Cake sounds about right."

"Better practice blowing, you two," Dot said to Miles and

Lucky, "to be sure you blow out all seventeen candles and get your wishes."

Lucky wished that wishing really worked. If it did, her wishes would be that Short Sammy's box had never arrived, that Paloma would be there for the party, and that Lincoln would not leave Hard Pan. And way in the back row of her wishes, slouched back there because it could probably never come true, was the one about her father. He had been married to both of her mothers: first to Brigitte in France before Lucky was born, and then to Lucille. They had both divorced him, one after the other, but they must have loved him too, at least at first. And he *must*—kind of, in his own way—love *her*, Lucky thought, because he had convinced Brigitte to come all the way from France to take care of her when she was eight and Lucille had died. He sent money every month and had helped Brigitte financially a little bit with starting up the Café. But even though *Lucky* hadn't divorced her father, he never saw her or talked to her or wrote to her, and she didn't understand why. And she wished she did understand, wished so strongly that it made her heart feel like a hard little forgotten scrunched-up ball of a washcloth with all the water squeezed out of it.

"My first wish," Miles said, pulling Lucky back from thoughts of her father, "was to have a great big Hard Pan party, and that wish is already coming true." He smiled the sweet way he did when you gave him a cookie, the way that made you give him a second one. Then he said something that echoed exactly what Lucky had been thinking. "My other ones are the kind of wishes where they never come true but you wish them anyway. Do you ever have those, Brigitte?"

"Of course," Brigitte said. "Adults have big, big wishes that we do not expect to come true. That is why we need so many more candles on our cakes."

Everyone laughed and started talking all at once about wishes, everyone except Lucky. Sometimes what wishes do, Lucky knew, especially the big, big wishes, is churn up all the confusion and longing that sloshes around forever inside of you.

11. hard pan astronomy

Lucky ate her s'more and listened to the others. But she didn't want some more, and she didn't laugh with them. She felt unseen, a lamp with its cord unplugged from the socket. No one really understood her, and partly the problem was that Lucky didn't understand *herself*. She knew that deep in her heart she loved her family and her extended family and the town where she lived. It was fine that Brigitte wasn't a regular sort of mother, and Lincoln wasn't a typical kind of friend, and Miles wasn't an actual little brother, and Short Sammy wasn't a real grandfather, and Dot and Mrs. Prender weren't blood-related family. But all of that was somehow not *enough*.

She leaned back and gazed up at the inky-black sky, crammed with stars. The moon looked like a happy-face smile on its side. "What I don't get," she said suddenly, "is the Milky Way."

"Our galaxy," Lincoln said, pointing at it with his metal skewer.

Everyone leaned their heads back to study the sky, which from this spot in their desert valley was like the inside of an immense black domed Weber lid. As if, Lucky thought, maybe God had a pesky second cousin once removed who'd played with the lid when she was a child, and she'd jabbed it a billion times from up above with her s'mores skewer. And we humans look up and see what we call stars, but really they are just bits of the immense light from beyond, shining through the jagged holes she made. If someone lifted that domed lid, the light would be so intense and so beautiful that all the people looking up would lie down on their backs, tears pouring out of their eyes, and die. Lucky decided to save this idea for later. It was the kind of strange and personal story that you couldn't go around telling to just anyone.

"The part about it that I don't get," Lucky said, "is—"

"The Milky part?" Lincoln asked. "Dust particles," he said, clasping his hands behind his head and leaning back into them.

"Not that," Lucky said. "What I don't get is how the Earth can be a member of the Milky Way galaxy when *we're* over here and *it* is zillions of light-years from us, out there. Plus, our whole solar system is here—I mean, look at Venus." Lucky pointed off to the side. "It's not even close to the Milky Way! So how does it work that we're *in* a galaxy that we're *not* in?"

"When we were kids we learned all the planets in the solar system in order," Dot said. "'My very efficient mother just sewed us new pants.'"

Everyone turned to stare at Dot. She had plenty of news and gossip flowing into and out of her back-porch beauty salon, a lot of stuff you could never Google, but sometimes what she said sounded a little bit off.

"It's how we remembered the placement," Dot explained. "Starting closest to the sun, you take the first letter of each word in the saying. My/Mercury very/Venus efficient/Earth mother/Mars just/Jupiter sewed/Saturn us/Uranus new/Neptune pants/Pluto."

"Pluto isn't a planet any longer, man," Short Sammy said. "They took it out a couple of years ago. Too small."

"That's not fair at *all*," said Miles, whose own smallness often made *him* feel left out.

"Well, plus it ruins the whole saying," Dot complained. "You can't say, 'My very efficient mother just sewed us new.' Doesn't make sense."

"Wait, but nobody even gets my question," Lucky said, "which is: How can the Milky Way be our *home*, and our solar system's home, when it's zillions of light-years away from us?"

There was a short silence as everyone thought this over. Then Mrs. Prender shouted, "It's like a fried egg."

"What is?" Miles asked.

"The Milky Way."

Short Sammy spoke up. "And the Earth is like a grain of salt in the fried egg."

Dot frowned and asked, "Where in the fried egg is the grain of salt?"

Short Sammy considered this. "In the yolk," he said.

"No, it would be in the white part," Dot reasoned. "The yolk would be the Black Hole."

"Then it's more like a doughnut than a fried egg," Short Sammy began, as he put the lid on the Weber and closed all the vents. "Saves the coals, man," he said to Brigitte. "They'll stop burning, and you can relight them next time."

Lucky had had enough of Hard Pan astronomy, which was confusing and not really about the Milky Way. She wished Paloma were there, so they could be by themselves and make their stomachs ache from laughing over fried eggs and black holes and doughnuts and Dot's very efficient mother. No one else would understand. Miles was too young, the adults were too old, and Lincoln was too serious.

The guests began gathering up their plastic cups and metal skewers, agreeing that they'd all had a wonderful time, Dot getting in a last word about dwarf planets and how Pluto should be allowed, someday, to rejoin the solar system.

"It's not that Pluto isn't in the solar system, man," Short Sammy explained. "It's just not an official planet any longer."

Lucky sighed. She helped Mrs. Prender find her flashlight in the bottom of the bag full of sticky skewers, uneaten graham crackers, and mushed-up marshmallows. Then everyone except Lincoln was leaving, following the thin blades of their flashlight beams to their cars.

As Lincoln helped Brigitte carry stuff inside, Lucky took the bag of trash around behind the trailers and dumped it in the bin. She stood there in the pool of light from the kitchen window, listening to Lincoln and Brigitte's laughter.

The "Way" in Milky Way doesn't mean "way" like in, *Here's the way to cook a marshmallow. Path* is what "Way" means. So, Lucky thought, instead of our Earth being a member of some other, easier galaxy, like the Clear Way or the Simple Way or the Turn Right at the Big Dipper Way, what we got for our very own home in the universe was a cloudy, confusing, smeared-milk Way. Lucky looked up at it again, so remote and distant, yet somehow our home.

HMS Beagle stood there, waiting to see if anything would drop out of the trash bin and to find out what would happen next. Lucky rubbed behind her dog's ear. "Beag, is your Way a clear, uncomplicated, simple, easy Way?"

HMS Beagle gazed back at her. Yes, with Lucky there, it was.

"Good," Lucky said. "Maybe, if I remember, I'll Google the galaxy tomorrow, see what's up."

HMS Beagle agreed, but she forgot all about it the next day, and so did Lucky.

12. fifty individual birthday cakes

All the Hard Panners who wanted to help Brigitte in her campaign to become more Californian and more American turned out to have a specialty. Short Sammy gave tips about American cooking, especially his technique of using bacon fat to improve taste. Dot advised on hair coloring, permanents, and jewelry, and the Captain explained about Harleys and Chevys. Miles and Lincoln continued coaching Brigitte on food and also useful idioms and slang, and Lucky offered many helpful suggestions on parenting.

Brigitte listened to all her advisers. She asked lots of questions. But often she smiled at the advice, and sometimes she actually burst out laughing. And even when Brigitte did follow the recommendations, deep down she still kept on being French.

After school on Tuesday, Brigitte, Lincoln, and Lucky sat around the kitchen trailer dinette, each working on a separate project. Brigitte leafed through one of her recipe books and blew air out of her lips like a horse. She did not have an oven big enough to bake a birthday cake for forty-three people. "How will I make a cake so enormous?" she asked Lucky and Lincoln. "Even American mothers in regular house-kitchens do not have such a big oven. To bake this big cake, what will they do, these American mothers?"

As she brushed clear nail polish on her toenails, Lucky thought about all the mothers in America making birthday cakes. Brigitte let her prop her feet up against the edge of the dinette table, like a contortionist in the circus, to bring her toes close enough for a proper job. Lucky's toes were short and stubby, but they grew in a very rare and beautiful alignment, with the big toes descending down to the little pinkies in a perfect line. No toe stuck out too far or was too short. Plus she had a delicate, high arch. For this reason, Lucky felt a little vain about her feet, and she was sorry Lincoln only saw the back of them from across the table. The bottoms of toes are entirely different, being on the nonpublic, hardworking side of the foot, and are interesting but not as gorgeous as the tops can be. "A lot of mothers would probably go to the store and buy a big sheet cake," she said.

"Sheet cakes are cool," Lincoln agreed, "because you can write a message on them, like 'Happy Birthday, Miles and Lucky.'" Lincoln had finally confirmed that his entry in the International Guild of Knot Tyers' contest was a type of net, but he wouldn't say what type, or anything else about it. Deep in her heart, Lucky hoped it wouldn't be a perfect net or even a great net, so that Lincoln would lose and have to stay in Hard Pan instead of going to England. He had hung a sawed-off broomstick horizontally from two hooks on the opposite wall of the trailer, about waist level, and by turning sideways from his seat on the banquette he could use this broomstick as an anchor for his net, as he wove and knotted strands of cord with a plastic, ruler-length tool. As the net grew bigger and bigger, it still looked to Lucky like a plain old fishing net.

Brigitte lifted one shoulder and made a little tongue-click sound. "Well, you know, we are not going to the store to buy this sheet cake, because there is no store and anyway, it would not be as good as a cake made at home. So, back to one square."

Lincoln turned to look at her for a moment. "You mean, 'back to square one.'"

"Yes, back to square one, of how to make this gigantic cake in a tiny oven."

67

"Maybe there's a way to make a bunch of small sheet cakes and somehow glue them all together invisibly," Lucky suggested.

Lincoln passed his plastic tool—he called it a needle but it didn't look *anything* like a needle—over and under some cord, forming diamond shapes, and said, "You could make forty-three cupcakes."

"Hmmm. Cupcakes," Brigitte said, frowning.

Lucky peered around her foot to slide her eyes sideways at Lincoln, who didn't look back at her. "You've heard of cupcakes, right?"

"Well, of course I hear of them," she said. "They are, if I remember, the little cakes you eat . . . out of a cup."

"Uh-uh," said Lucky. Brigitte knew the difference between *uh-huh* and *uh-uh* when she heard it, but she always got them confused when she was talking, so you were never sure if she meant no or yes. Lincoln had worked with her on *uh-huh* and *uh-uh* extensively, but she couldn't get it. "Little individual cakes in their own pleated paper holder, with frosting on top. You don't even need a plate or a fork to eat them."

Lincoln pulled a cord carefully into place and said, "With cupcakes, you should make some extras, just in case people want another one." Lincoln had gotten into a phase where he was always ravenous. To Lucky, he seemed to eat enough for about three people. He had a fast metabolism, which meant, as far as Lucky could figure it, that his organs passed around the ingredients in the food and zipped them through his corpuscles instantly, while regular people's corpuscles took their time. His fast metabolism was why Lincoln didn't get fat, no matter how much he ate.

"Every person," Brigitte said, "each with our own little cake."

Lucky surveyed her toes, all ten of them in excellent proportion to one another, all shining with clear nail polish. She'd only gotten a little bit of polish on the skin around them, and you couldn't really see it unless you got up close. And most people fortunately didn't go around putting their faces right next to people's feet in order to examine how neat their nail polish was. She leaned forward and blew on them to make them dry quicker.

Brigitte closed her cookbook and rested her chin on the heel of her hand. "This cupcake is another wonderful American invention," she said.

Lucky fanned her toes apart in a way that Brigitte (Lucky had earlier discovered) could not do with her own long, fingerlike toes. Toe spreading is like lengthwise tongue curling, single-eyebrow raising, and ear wiggling—either you can do it or you can't, no matter how hard you try. It's up to your DNA as to whether or not you have these talents. Lucky herself had all of them. "You'll have to get cupcake tins to bake them in," she said.

"I am sure we will find them at the thrift shop," Brigitte said, "or we can borrow them. We will take a picture, because no one in France will believe I make forty-three cakes for this birthday. They will see how American I am becoming."

"I'd say, probably we'll need about fifty," Lincoln put in.

If Paloma were there, Lucky thought, they would be exchanging eye-shrugs and secret don't-make-me-laugh looks, finding all the weird and funny stuff no one else saw. Sometimes that happened with Lincoln, but right now he was off in some other thought, and for once he stopped working on his net. He grinned at Brigitte in a delighted kind of way, which sent a jolt through Lucky's brain stem. Even though Lucky had recently realized she'd rather have Paloma than Lincoln as her best friend, it hadn't occurred to her that he would ever feel differently about *her*. All their lives Lucky had known that a part of Lincoln loved her; he couldn't help it. He would always love her, no matter what; she took that for granted. But at that moment he was looking at Brigitte.

"A digital picture to send by e-mail," Brigitte said. She pronounced "digital" in her French way, "dee-gee-tal," each syllable crisp, like a freshly ironed shirt. Freshly ironed clothes were a rarity in Hard Pan; they caught your eye. Brigitte's accent was like that: out of place, and yet pleasing; it caught your ear. "Lincoln, look at your net!" Brigitte said suddenly. "It is becoming so big and quite beautiful. What, I wonder, will you catch in it?"

Lucky shifted into a regular seated position by putting her beautiful, ignored feet under the table. No one had noticed her perfectly aligned toes or her unusual ability to spread them out as if they were fingers. Her excellent sheet cake idea had been tossed out the window. She might as well not even be sitting there, even though it was all about *her* birthday. Worse, Lincoln seemed preoccupied with useless things that had nothing to do with her. His knot tying wasn't just a peculiar hobby any longer—he'd become so good that he had made friends with the most famous knot-man in England, and he was showered with praise by Brigitte, and probably he would win that contest. Then he would leave Hard Pan, which had suddenly become puny and unimportant to him, Lucky realized, a stupid little place that didn't even show up on most maps.

So when Lincoln packed up his net, folding it into the plastic bag on the floor, and went outside with Brigitte to pinch off some herbs to take to his mom, Lucky stood and gazed for a moment at the everything drawer; then she yanked it open. It contained abandoned stuff that might still be useful: bottle stoppers and spools of twine and corks and rubber bands. It also held a pair of sharp, long-bladed scissors; Lucky snatched them. Squatting down by the plastic bag, she pulled it open and plunged her scissor-hand inside. Then she made three quick cuts in different random places on the net.

Lucky slammed the scissors back in the drawer and stood in the doorway, taking deep breaths. She smelled dill and cilantro and thyme, fresh and clean, strong in the air. She tried to explain to herself why she had secretly cut Lincoln's net. She tried to make a good reason in her mind. It was like a sudden illness, as if her meanness gland had swelled up and pumped nasty corpuscles throughout her bloodstream.

The meanness in her bloodstream made her skin feel sticky and her scalp grubby. Lucky imagined peeling off her grimy skin and throwing it into the washing machine.

There were red marks on her thumb and forefinger, where she'd gripped the scissors. She hid the marks with her other hand, and she hid her meanness deep in the laundry hamper of her heart.

13. a decision to trust

As she lay on her bed copying a map of the solar system for science homework on Tuesday evening, Lucky listened to Brigitte's end of a phone conversation with Paloma's mom, whose name turned out to be Carmen. It was their second long talk.

Brigitte had filled Lucky in about Mrs. Wellborne's worries from their first phone call. She worried about bugs and infections and bacteria and dust and wild animals and rabid dogs and kids who might be bad influences and Paloma's homework and, especially, she worried about people she called Old Desert Rat Characters. Carmen wondered why the Old Desert Rat Characters would live in such a remote place for years and years; why they didn't want to be closer to civilization, and what they did with their time, way out there in the desert. Lucky wasn't sure, but she thought probably Short Sammy and the Captain and Dot and Mrs. Prender were all Old Desert Rat Characters. Brigitte said quietly, "I suppose we are living here because this is our home."

It was obvious to Lucky from Brigitte's tone of voice during this second conversation that she was worn out reassuring Mrs. Wellborne. Finally Brigitte said, "I tell you something, Carmen. The whole world is full of danger. But also it is full of beauty and courage and many wonders. We both have the daughter to protect, but if we protect a little bit too much, they do not realize that we trust them to make good choices and to be brave. Sometimes they make the little mistake, and that is one way they learn. So you have to decide to trust or do not trust."

In her canned-ham trailer, where she was listening through the open doorway, Lucky hugged HMS Beagle. It was a splendissimo speech and Lucky was positive that Carmen, having already allowed Paloma to visit Hard Pan once, would decide to trust. And since she felt so triumphant, Lucky didn't know why, suddenly, she was crying into the Beag's silky coat. Silently, so Brigitte wouldn't hear, Lucky held on and cried and stroked the Beag, stroked and stroked her warm coat until the hard metallic phantom sensation of scissors against her skin finally went away. Then Lucky released her dog and stretched up the neck of her nightgown to press it hard against her eyes. And she made herself envision the vast timelessness of space, where trust is only a tiny speck, practically invisible, lost and all but unimportant in the infinity of the universe.

Feeling weary, Lucky picked up her notebook again and penciled in the three dwarf planets and an assortment of asteroids and meteoroids, labeling them "small bodies," which is the official scientific term. It was a big family, the solar system, with all those other planets' moons, way over a hundred of them, but she only showed our own moon, a tiny circle. She shaded in Jupiter, which is huge and uninhabitable for humans. Lucky often wondered if there were other planets not in our solar system but somewhere in our own galaxy, the far-off Milky Way, with nice weather and drinking water and lots of animals adapted to their habitats like on Earth. Sometimes she *longed* for there to be another planet somewhere, like ours. The idea of the Earth being the only planet with life in the whole universe became, to Lucky at that moment, unbearably lonely and sad.

Brigitte was saying, "Yes, the girls sleep in the trailer—Paloma can have Lucky's bed and I make a little bed on the floor for Lucky. No, no, it is fine. No, the dog has not fleas. . . ." Lucky rolled her eyes to herself. If dogs could roll their eyes, Lucky was sure that HMS Beagle would do so too.

Lucky would have jumped on a rocket, with no hesitation, to go to another planet and see the life on it, but Mrs. Wellborne was afraid of a little town in the desert, where nothing bad could possibly happen.

14. chesterfield

In the middle of the night, a noise—so loud and close that it jolted the canned-ham trailer—made Lucky sit bolt upright. HMS Beagle bounded to the door. Seconds later Brigitte flew in, leaped on the bed, and grabbed Lucky in both her arms. The noise—neither human nor machine—blasted into the trailer again. It sounded like an enormous giant jumping on the creaky, rusty metal bedsprings of an old bed with no mattress. Up and down the giant jumped, ancient metal shrieking into an amplified microphone. Brigitte held on tighter, and Lucky could feel her heart pounding.

"What is this terrible sound?" Brigitte whispered.

Lucky had heard it before, though never from so close. "It's a burro," she said.

Brigitte loosened her grip. Lucky's eyes were getting used to the dark, and she could see Brigitte's scared-looking face by the moonlight through the window. Even after living there more than two years, Brigitte found life in the high desert mysterious and sometimes threatening.

"What is he doing here?" she asked, already going from scared to mad. "This burro should not be in our yard."

Lucky smiled to herself. "It probably thinks *we're* in *its* yard." She stood and went to the porthole window. "Don't turn on the light—come see." She gestured to Brigitte to join her. HMS Beagle had her nose to the crack under the door, sniffing. She looked from Lucky to the door and back, asking to be allowed to go out and run off the intruder. "Shhhh," Lucky said, her signal to the Beag not to bark.

The burro was meandering around the Café tables but stopped when it came to Brigitte's potted herb and lettuce garden.

Brigitte put her face next to Lucky's in order to look out of the tiny window. "He is going to eat my vegetables!" she said in an outraged whisper.

Lucky wanted to stay quiet and watch. She had a perfect view of the whole yard. Right away, she liked this burro. Its belly sagged and its coat was very shaggy, which made it look old and kind of run-down. One ear tilted way out to the side, on a head that looked enormous in proportion to its smallish body. A breeze blew its scent, which was grassy and horsey, into the trailer.

"I am going to frighten him away," Brigitte said. "He has not the right to eat my parsley!"

"Wait." Lucky stalled for time. "Let's see what happens. He reminds me of Chesterfield."

It was interesting that the short-legged animal, who was maybe only half as big as a regular horse, had such a huge head, ears, and voice. Lucky decided that he looked more like a really ragged pet than a wild creature.

"And who is this Chesterfield?" Brigitte asked. "I do not know him."

"Just a made-up burro in stories I tell Miles."

The burro's ears swiveled toward them, and he turned his head in their direction.

"Shhhh," Lucky said again very quietly.

The burro raised his lips and opened his mouth, showing very large and yellowish teeth. He brayed again, straight at the window.

"Why do I whisper when he is yelling insults at me?" demanded Brigitte.

Just then, the burro began to pee. A huge stream of urine shot out with such force that it gouged a trench in the sandy topsoil. Lucky watched with interest, gripping Brigitte's hand to keep her there. He went on peeing and peeing. A pee-lake started to form. As a scientist, Lucky wished she could measure exactly the quantity of pee and the time it took. It was very surprisingly and wondrously a *lot*.

Brigitte wrenched her hand out of Lucky's and stamped into the kitchen, where she grabbed the flyswatter. Lucky was on her heels.

"Brigitte, what are you going to do?"

"Swat that big nuisance and make him go away! He peed in our Café!"

"No! He'll kick you! He could break your leg!" Lucky had no idea if this was true, but she wanted Brigitte to leave him alone. Maybe she could make friends with him. She imagined saying to Paloma, *Oh, look, here comes Chesterfield. He's wild, but he kind of likes to hang out here.* She could see Paloma's expression, and how cool Paloma would think it was to have a wild burro as a friend. Also, she knew Paloma would *die* of laughter if she ever got to see Chesterfield pee.

"I am not afraid of that beast," Brigitte said unconvincingly.

Lucky clicked her tongue and shook her head in a professional-desert-resident way. In certain cases with Brigitte it was important for Lucky to act like she had total command of the situation. "He'd become loco the minute he saw that flyswatter, Brigitte," Lucky improvised. "It's common knowledge around here. You *never* want a burro to catch sight of a flyswatter or any other sort of flapping thing in your hand. Just let me handle this."

"You will not go out there!" Brigitte exclaimed.

As if she were concentrating too hard to hear, Lucky opened the fridge, grabbed a carrot and an apple, and mumbled, "This should work," like she was an experienced burro expert dealing with a situation that she would soon have well under control. HMS Beagle went to stand at the kitchen door.

"You stay here, Beag," Lucky said in a strict voice, and gave her dog the carrot. "That burro might think you're a coyote." To Brigitte she said, "Don't worry; I know what I'm doing. Please keep HMS Beagle inside."

Lucky had often allowed Brigitte to think that her adopted daughter had more experience than was actually the case. This came in very handy, time after time. Brigitte said, "His teeth will bite off your fingers!"

But Lucky, barefoot and wearing her warm-weather nightie, slipped out quickly, closing the door behind her.

Brigitte wrenched it open immediately, but stayed in the doorway.

Instead of looking straight at the animal, Lucky turned her face to the side because she knew that non-meat-eaters, like the burro, do not like it when meat-eaters, like Lucky, look at them directly. His own eyes, outlined in white, were slanted up in a way that made him look sleepy and sweet. Lucky scratched the skin of the apple with her fingernail, releasing its apple smell.

She walked, slowly, to the closest Café table and put the apple on it.

"Here you go, Chesterfield," she said in a soft voice. "You can have the apple but not Brigitte's parsley or vegetables." She could hear Brigitte's breathy *pfft* of disbelief behind her.

The burro twitched its scraggly tail. Dust floated off its thick, patchy-looking coat in the moonlight. Up this close, even viewed from the corners of Lucky's eyes, he was a really dilapidated burro, probably old enough to be a great-grandfather. Everything about him was tough and worn and dried out except his gentle, long-eyelashed eyes and his white velvety muzzle.

Lucky glanced back at the kitchen trailer doorway. Brigitte, wearing the oversize T-shirt she slept in, clutching the flyswatter, did not take her eyes off the burro.

Lucky sighed. It was good that, like Lincoln, Brigitte and the Beag watched out for her, but at the same time too bad none of them realized how strong and swift and smart she was in dangerous situations. They didn't know how much like Charles Darwin she was. Just like him, she would have tons of adventures, make important discoveries, and live to be very, very old. She could take care of herself.

Chesterfield put his great head to the ground for a moment, then slowly turned and wandered off toward the open desert on neat tiny hooves. Lucky watched him awhile, then came inside, feeling disappointed.

HMS Beagle sniffed her thoroughly, sneezed, and went to curl up on the little rug by Lucky's bed. Brigitte drank a tall glass of water, still watching out the kitchen window.

In the morning the apple was gone.

15. danger

HMS Beagle and Lucky were examining the burro's hoofprints in the early morning light when Brigitte called, "There is e-mail for you!" and Lucky ran into the kitchen where the Dell laptop was open. Brigitte gave Lucky her place at the little built-in table. "Please do not take too long—I have some reservations for the weekend to answer, and also orders to make."

The weekend meant customers, and Brigitte was ordering some meat and vegetable deliveries over the Internet. Lucky slid into the seat.

"Dear Luck," she read. "Mom said yes! C U Friday!!!!! P.S. Have you learned to swim yet? Xxx Pal."

Lucky yipped and raised her two fists. "Her mom said yes!" she told Brigitte.

"Because I promise her on the telephone you two girls will be careful. She does not really know us, and she is very, very worried about Paloma's safety." Brigitte gestured toward the miles and miles of Mojave Desert outside. She put her hands on each side of Lucky's face and leaned over, zinging waves of seriousness straight out of her eyes and straight into Lucky's. *"Ma puce,"* she said in her deep, quiet voice, "you must be thinking always about this and not get into even a little bit of trouble or she will never let Paloma come back."

"I know," said Lucky, and made her own eyes gaze back at Brigitte, beaming a 100 percent promise that trouble was the *last* thing she and Paloma would get into. Brigitte let her go, and Lucky clicked on Reply. "Dear Pal, YAY!!!!!!" she typed. "P.S. Plastic bucket big enuf for both to learn to swim. Treading water until Friday. C U xxx Luck."

But a little later, Lucky had another e-mail. "Uncle Rocky can't get away this weekend. I cried so hard my mom and dad decided to bring me themselves. Bad mistake!!!!!!! Now we R stuck! Xxx Pal."

Lucky puzzled over this message. Paloma hadn't talked much about her parents except to say her father was in the Industry, which she explained meant he had something to do with the movies, and that her mom had been a child actress but no one famous, just commercials and parts on TV. To Lucky they sounded interesting and gorgeous, and she wondered why Paloma didn't want them to come to Hard Pan.

One thing she remembered was that Paloma said her mother listened in on her phone calls and wouldn't let her have her own cell. Lucky had laughed and said cell phones didn't work in Hard Pan because of the mountains and hills all around, so she didn't have one either.

Lucky resolved to make a good impression on Paloma's parents by being conscientious, careful, and well behaved. And Hard Pan would be the most safe and perfect place for kids to be, with no danger whatsoever. That way they would allow Paloma to visit often on weekends. And if Lucky and Paloma did have some adventures, they would just be careful that no one found out.

But deep in the crevices of her mind, worried thoughts of Paloma's mother and father wormed around day and night.

That was why, on the bus ride to school, Lucky imagined herself to *be* Paloma's parents. Next to her, Miles was hunched over *Brain Surgery for Beginners*. Even though he had to sound out, aloud, some of the words (a very tedious experience for Lucky to endure), he pressed on. And he talked endlessly about brains.

Lincoln was holding *Knot News* in one hand and two cords in the other. Lucky's eyes, now with Paloma's parents' minds superimposed over her own mind, saw both boys in a new way. Instead of his usual comfortable self, Lincoln seemed abnormal. Maybe even *sub*normal. "Can't you ever *not* knot?" she asked him suddenly.

Lincoln looked surprised. Lucky knew that even his teachers had tried to get him to quit knotting in class ever since second grade, but they gave up when he got As in everything

whether he knotted or not. "This issue of *Knot News* is about repairing tears in a net," he said, as if that answered her question, looking straight at her in his level, open way. "And this," he went on, "is a double fisherman's knot. It's handy if you need a weight-bearing knot to join two different cords."

"Lincoln, that's just it. I *don't* need one." Lucky had never lied to Lincoln, but now she pretended not to know why he was reading an article about repairing tears. One of her brain crevices told her that it wasn't really lying if you didn't actually say anything. But right behind her eyes, Lucky felt a hot finger of shame pressing on her tear ducts.

Lincoln raised his eyebrows at her as if she had completely missed the point. "Between you and eternity could be the right knot," he said.

The grown-up-ness of this answer, and the calm, kind way he said it, and the hard-to-get-ness of its meaning irritated Lucky, which was a relief because it made her stop feeling like crying. An image popped into her mind of Mount Rushmore, with its four presidents carved out of the stone mountain, looking wise and strong and forever. She pictured Lincoln's face chiseled up there with them. Okay, fine, she thought, but couldn't Lincoln just be a *little* more like other kids, just a bit more normal? Lincoln didn't even talk like a regular person.

Miles, in his own way, was even worse. His hair looked as if it had never been combed, which was more or less true; his face was smeared with traces of cookies, his fingers were sticky—the fingernails black—and his pants were shiny-dark on the sides where he rubbed his hands. He would definitely give Paloma's parents a very bad impression.

It would be impossible, even for Lucky, to reform both Lincoln and Miles in one day, so the only solution was to keep Paloma's parents from meeting them at all.

When Sandi the bus driver pulled up in the town of Dale and made five little kids hurry up and get in their seats so she could stay on schedule, Lucky looked out the window and said casually, "Paloma's coming back tomorrow to stay for the weekend."

"Oh, good," said Miles, who had mooched several cookies off her. "Maybe Chesterfield will even come back and pee again, and I bet Paloma'll laugh so much she won't be able to stand up." Miles had heard the whole story of the burro's visit while they'd waited for the bus. He'd made Lucky promise to call him on the phone, any time, day or night, if Chesterfield showed up again.

Lincoln concentrated on his knot, looking back and forth from a series of complicated-looking diagrams in *Knot News*.

"But her parents are coming too, and from what I hear you two probably better not come around."

"How come?" asked Lincoln, glancing up at her.

"They're—worrywarts," Lucky said, which was true. Then she began improvising. "They're kind of scared of children. . . ." She realized that their own daughter was a child, and corrected herself. "I mean, they're scared of *boys*."

"Why?" Miles asked.

"Danger," Lucky said after a pause.

"What kind of danger?" Miles looked extremely fascinated by this subject.

Lucky wished she'd thought this out ahead of time. "Well," she said, "this boy told a lie about Carmen, that's Paloma's mom, and got her in trouble when she was exactly Paloma's age."

"What lie did he tell?"

"It's a . . . secret," said Lucky. "Even Paloma doesn't know for sure."

Lincoln had his head to one side, gazing at a corner of the bus. "I'm trying to think what kind of lie would be so dangerous," he said.

"All Paloma knows is that her mom almost died. So now as a parent she's very strict and won't even let Pal have a cell phone."

Lincoln gave Lucky an odd look, which she ignored.

"What happens is, lots of times when Carmen sees boys, she remembers the terrible lie from when she was a child and sometimes—she can't help herself—she even *bites* them. She bites their earlobes, really hard—I'm talking about *absolute strangers*—grabbing them with her teeth and not letting go. Especially boys between six and twelve."

Lucky paused to assess how well her story was working as a way to make Lincoln and Miles stay away from Paloma's parents. Miles looked impressed and a bit fearful. Lincoln was only gazing at her with a little smile, like someone waiting for the punch line of a joke.

"So if you want to come over, well, that would be okay as far as Paloma and I go, but it might"—here Lucky got a great inspiration—"it *could* really upset Brigitte, she being a brand-new official mother. It could give her a very bad example of parenting. Before that, she'd never even have *thought* of biting boys' earlobes. But once she sees it . . ." Lucky sighed deeply and shook her head.

"You mean you think that could make *Brigitte* start biting boys' earlobes?" asked Miles in horror.

They had nearly arrived in Sierra City by then, and Lucky was glad. Her story was good, she thought, in general, having intrigue, excitement, and tragedy, but it wasn't quite working with Lincoln. "Who knows for sure?" she said. "Brigitte is really feeling her way along as far as being a mom. A lot of trial and error. I don't think it would be good for her at all to see that kind of behavior in another mom. In my opinion, just for this weekend, maybe boys should keep their distance."

Lucky started pulling on the straps of her backpack. "That's just my opinion," she repeated, and shrugged in a but-it's-entirely-up-to-you way.

Miles said, "*I'm* going to stay far enough away so she can't catch me and bite my earlobes, and if she tries, I'll bite *hers*."

Lucky saw that she had more embellishing to do on the story, especially when Lincoln Clinton Carter Kennedy, possible future president of the United States, *Knot News* under one arm and the giant black plastic bag slung over his back, climbed down the steps of the bus, laughing.

16. a jackhammer

The mail truck pulled up at the Hard Pan post office each week-day at ten fifteen, and everyone hung around outside, waiting for the Captain to distribute the mail to the P.O. boxes. This gave people a chance to get the latest news and check around to see who might have whatever they needed to borrow.

When HMS Beagle and Brigitte met Lucky at the bus drop-off after school, and Lincoln and Miles went in search of a soccer ball, Lucky discovered that Chesterfield had visited more than one Hard Pan resident. Brigitte reported what she'd heard at the post office that morning.

It turned out that the burro was front-page headlines in Hard Pan, and it wasn't his first visit. He'd come around before but usually didn't bray; normally he was pretty silent. Some people were concerned that he would eat their gardens or destroy their property, others were worried that he would bring some weird disease-carrying flies into town, and everyone agreed that his braying this time was loud enough to raise the dead.

Short Sammy, who Lucky felt sure would have defended Chesterfield, had been at work during this post office discussion, clearing litter from his adopted highway. But his absence gave the other residents a chance to compare notes on Sammy's mysterious box once the topic of the burro had been thoroughly hashed over.

"I am going to speak to him about this," Brigitte told Lucky now as they walked toward home along the deserted main road. "To everyone who ask him, Sammy will say only that it is a surprise. But I want to be sure he is okay."

"Maybe it's some kind of musical instrument," Lucky said, thinking of how much Short Sammy enjoyed playing his guitar, wanting the box not to be a casket.

"*Non.* It cannot be a musical instrument."

"Why not?"

Instead of taking the short cut across the rear of the Captain's property, vacant lots sprouting low bushes, they continued walking the long way, on the paved street. Brigitte met Lucky at the bus stop most days if it wasn't too hot, so she could use up calories as a way of not getting fat.

"Because he ask to borrow the jackhammer of Klincke Ken." Klincke Ken lived on disability, which meant he got a check every month on account of his bad back and not being able to get a job. Lucky figured his parents must have been kind of confused, because his first name, which you pronounced "Clinky," sounded like some brand of tool, and his last name, Ken, made you think it was a first name. Anyway, no one ever called him plain Klincke or plain Ken, they always called him by both names, Klincke Ken. Before his back went bad, Klincke Ken had been a handyman-carpenter, and he still had a shed filled with tools that he loaned out to people in exchange for a six-pack of Bud Light or a homemade pie.

"What's Short Sammy need a jackhammer for?" Lucky asked.

"This is what Klincke Ken ask him. Sammy says it is to dig a hole."

Lucky knew that under a thin layer of loose sand, the ground in Hard Pan was as hard as cement. You couldn't dig a hole in the normal way, with a shovel. You needed a jackhammer.

Lucky speeded up until she got in front of Brigitte, then turned around and continued walking backward so she could look directly into Brigitte's face. "So maybe he has some kind of planter inside the box and he's going to sink it halfway in the ground, like he said at the barbecue. Maybe he's figured out a way to keep the cottontails from eating his chili peppers if they're planted in a container," she said, as HMS Beagle zigzagged between them, figuring this was a new game.

"Maybe," said Brigitte, lifting one shoulder slightly.

Lucky saw what she had suspected on Brigitte's face: worry.

"What?" said Lucky. "You think he's digging a grave?"

"This is what some people think. But I do not know. Short Sammy seems very . . . what is the word . . . enthusiast?"

"Enthusiastic?"

"Yes, not like a sad man who digs his own grave beside his front door. It is very strange. I will take him some radish-leaf soup later and ask him."

"I'll go with you," Lucky said.

"*Non*, Lucky. I want to talk with Sammy alone."

Lucky did not understand why adults were always trying to keep important information from kids. It was very frustrating, because it made kids have to work twice as hard to find things out.

91

Lucky faced front again, toward home: their three trailers, connected in a way that curved slightly, like the curve of Brigitte's arm as she put it around Lucky's shoulders. HMS Beagle trotted along on Lucky's other side, their three shadows entwined as each one silently thought her own thoughts.

17. a good impression

As far as Lucky was concerned, running a café—even one only open on weekends and holidays—was harder than competing in the Badwater to Mount Whitney Ultramarathon, which is a very, very extreme sport. People don't realize that the cook, and especially the cook's *helper,* aren't just casually stirring something in a pan on the stove and then putting it on a plate, easy-breezy. No, back there in the kitchen there is a *lot* of *work.* By the time the Hard Pan Café had been open a few months, you could see the muscles in Brigitte's arms and legs, and even in her hands and fingers. She seemed to love the hard work. And Lucky, with the important job of assistant prep chef and busgirl, learned to wash, chop, slice, mash, measure, mince, grate, grind, set, serve, and clear.

One of Brigitte's handy tips that she taught Lucky is that certain dishes can be made ahead, which is a huge advantage to anyone in the café business. Things like soups and some desserts and salads. So Brigitte and Lucky had prepped as much as they could in advance (no snails or anything gross) and were ready for lots of customers to come on the weekend. But Lucky was nervous about Paloma's parents' visit. Certain things that have nothing to do with cooking, like making a good impression, you can only *try* to prep for in advance and then hope for the best.

On Friday afternoon Lucky sped outside to meet the Wellbornes the minute Paloma's father pulled up in a gigantic khaki-colored Hummer. Their vehicle looked like something made to transport a small army into a war zone. As Paloma's mom dismounted, gingerly taking the long step down to the ground in high-heeled shoes, Lucky inspected her. She wore loose cotton slacks with a matching pale gray silky shirt, a scarf that looked as gossamer as butterfly wings draped loosely around her neck, and delicate, spicy-smelling perfume. A perfect tiny row of wrinkles curved up at the sides of her eyes, showing that Mrs. Wellborne had done quite a lot of laughing in her life, and two deep lines between her eyebrows let you know (which Lucky already did thoroughly know) that she had also put in some serious time worrying.

As Paloma jumped out of the back, her mother called, "Paloma! Don't forget your wellness kit! Zeke, tell Paloma she *must* remember to keep herself safe!"

Paloma's father, emerging from the driver's side, waved a hand to show that he was busy with his mobile phone. Brigitte emerged from the kitchen trailer, smiling her big welcome.

Hoisting up a small pink backpack, Paloma said, "Mom,

I *am* safe," and, in a grown-up way that Lucky admired, introduced everyone.

As the two moms talked, Paloma looped an arm over Lucky's shoulder and said, "Listen, can you lend me thirty-nine dollars and ninety-five cents?" which made Lucky choke, cough, and laugh all at the same time, because—being exactly the price of learning to swim at home—it was a special coded way of talking that only Lucky would understand. Lucky got the hiccups, and Paloma had to pat her on the back. One unlucky hiccup was so loud and deep, as if coming from a huge man, that it surprised everyone, and Lucky knew that Paloma's esophagus had to make a giant effort to cram back its own laughter. Paloma mashed her forehead against Lucky's arm, making tiny spurting snorts.

Mrs. Wellborne was saying, "Brigitte, just look at this Café! Right in the middle of the desert, and yet it's like we arrived in the south of France! Oh, I wish we could stay for lunch!"

"Of course you must stay for lunch," Brigitte said. "You are our guests."

But Mr. Wellborne reported that his cell phone didn't work, frowning as if he'd found a tomato worm in his salad. Lucky and Paloma were still laughing and hiccuping, and then they leaned against the Hummer and got road dust all over themselves, which made Paloma start coughing, so Brigitte suggested that everyone sit at a table in the shade and have something cold to drink. She caught Lucky's eye and raised one eyebrow a teeny

bit, which made Lucky
suddenly remember that
she was supposed to be
giving the Wellbornes a
good impression.

"Zeke, I *told* you
there's no cell reception
here," Mrs. Wellborne said, her sides-of-the-eyes wrinkles and
her between-eyebrows wrinkles all scrunching up at once. She
turned back to Brigitte. "That's part of why I've been so worried
about Paloma staying—it's just so *remote* here. I keep envision-
ing some kind of terrible emergency. But meeting you and seeing what you've been able to do with this darling Café—"

"Honey, I don't remember you telling me that," Mr.
Wellborne interrupted. "And I think I *would* remember if
you had, because I have a studio conference call in five minutes! Where's the nearest Starbucks?"

Lucky became uneasy. This was not giving the Wellbornes
a good impression. It was a bad mark against the town that there
was no cell reception or Starbucks. "We don't have a Starbucks,"
Lucky said, "but you could use our landline," she added, avoiding
Brigitte's eye. She knew Brigitte kept the phone open so customers
could call to make a reservation or ask for directions. Lucky
moved closer to Brigitte and gave her a private, hard little poke.

"Yes, please come inside," Brigitte said after a moment, and
turned toward the kitchen trailer.

Mr. Wellborne cleared his throat and looked at his watch, which was to Brigitte's watch what the Hummer was to Brigitte's Jeep. "I'm afraid this is a *confidential* call," he said.

Brigitte turned back and gave Mr. Wellborne the beautiful, deep gaze that Lucky knew from experience meant serious business. That gaze could pin you to your chair and bore straight into the special deep compartments in your mind where you kept your bad thoughts. Mr. Wellborne was going to be in big trouble in a minute if he kept on with that attitude. Lucky grabbed Brigitte's hand and thought-beamed urgent pleas to let him off the hook. Brigitte relented.

"Please come in and use the phone, Mr. Wellborne," she said in a calm, steady voice. "I am sure you will not take long. It is the phone for my business. We will wait outside."

"Well . . . thank you," said Mr. Wellborne. The words sounded rusty, like some old metal tools he'd left outside and hadn't used in a long time. "I'm . . . sorry to be in such a rush."

He was rewarded with Brigitte's smile. "You are welcome, Mr. Wellborne," she said, and led him inside.

Lucky could hardly wait to get safely away with Paloma, but there was the problem of Mrs. Wellborne. It would be impolite to leave her sitting at the Café table by herself, yet Lucky was afraid that Mrs. Wellborne would start in again about all the bad things that could happen in Hard Pan.

Suddenly a breeze came up, grabbed Mrs. Wellborne's scarf, and tossed it like a leaf over and behind the half circle of trailers. "My scarf!" she cried. "Did you see that? The wind just yanked it off! It's probably halfway across the desert by now."

"We'll find it," Lucky said, with a meaningful look at Paloma. As Brigitte came out carrying glasses and a pitcher of water, the girls dashed behind the trailers to look for the scarf.

"It could be all the way up to the Found Object Wind Chime Museum already," Lucky suggested, thinking they could make the scarf search last a couple of hours if they were careful not to really look for it.

"Yeah, but we better not shilly-shally," Paloma said, reading Lucky's mind and letting her big smile out, "which, after we find it, we can figure out how to escape."

"Your mom is so gorgeous," Lucky said. She spotted the scarf on a low branch of a feathery-leaved mesquite tree by the dry wash, where it looked almost as beautiful, she thought, as around Mrs. Wellborne's throat.

"So's yours," Paloma said. "I just wish mine didn't worry so much. And I wish my dad—"

"Listen," Lucky interrupted, plucking the scarf off its branch. The subject of fathers was too complicated to go into right then. "We really should go up to the museum. Don't you want to see the other Paloma's brooch? We can get Sammy to tell the whole story of how she was tragically murdered."

Paloma put her finger across her lips. "Don't say that! My mom will freak out!"

Lucky nodded, remembering again her resolve to give the Wellbornes a good impression. "Okay, you're right," she said. "Let's go back."

But when they returned to the Café side of the trailers, Lucky saw something that she was sure would ruin all her plans.

18. anything is possible

Miles and Lincoln, those doorknobs! They were sitting at the table with Mrs. Wellborne and Brigitte. They had come down the dry wash just as Lucky and Paloma had gone scarf hunting around the other side of the trailers.

Lucky steamed toward them full speed, to do damage control and send them packing. A lot of bad impressions could result if she didn't act fast.

"It's sad about that thing that happened," Miles was saying as he leaned in toward Mrs. Wellborne. Lucky watched him sniffing her perfume and very subtly touching the fabric of her blouse. It was clear that Miles was entranced.

Brigitte gave Miles a quizzical glance and raised her eyebrows at Lucky. Lincoln seemed absorbed in tying a knot, but he also shot her a look. Lucky ignored them. "Here's your scarf, Mrs. Wellborne," she said in a way that was smooth and sweet, like spreading jam on a piece of bread. "It was hanging very nicely on the mesquite tree. I could show you the mesquite tree right now, since Miles and Lincoln were just going home."

"Thank you, dear," Mrs. Wellborne said, looking at Miles. Miles gazed back at her with his chocolate-chip eyes and smiled his dear, tender, cookie-mooching smile. He said, "You don't really need to be scared of b—"

Lucky cut him off. "Mrs. Wellborne just had a long car trip. I bet she'd really like some sun tea with lots of ice in it."

"*I* sure would," put in Paloma.

Brigitte looked at her watch. "We are waiting outside until Mr. Wellborne finishes his private telephone call. We will get the tea after."

"Miles was asking about when Mrs. Wellborne was a child," Lincoln said.

Mrs. Wellborne looked pleased. "A long time ago," she said, and then, laughing, "but not *that* long ago."

Lucky glared at Miles, who big-eyed her as a way of saying *he* wasn't doing anything wrong, and anyway Mrs. Wellborne was acting perfectly nice.

"My mom had lots of adventures," Paloma said, "when she was your age, Miles."

"But that was before—" Miles stopped suddenly. His hands flew to his earlobes as Lucky saw realization flash across his face.

"Yes, before I grew up and had a child of my own," Mrs. Wellborne said. "Then I found out that the world is full of danger, especially for children."

"Yes, it is," Lincoln said, to Lucky's annoyance. She gnashed her teeth mentally: The idea here was to reassure Paloma's mom, not *agree* with her. He shifted his big plastic trash bag. "That's one reason I'm trying to learn the right knot for every occasion." Lucky's mouth fell open. She'd never heard Lincoln even come close to bragging before. What was wrong with him? Then she realized: He was trying to impress Mrs. Wellborne!

Lucky watched Paloma's mother's rows of smile-wrinkles deepen; they were like a special decoration especially designed for her face. "Really?" she said. "How remarkable! Although when you think about it"—she switched to worry lines or, Lucky thought, maybe concentration lines—"how often would knots really be that useful?"

"Well," Lincoln said, "you could use the Josephine Knot on that scarf—it's a nice loose knot and has the advantage of being easily untied and tied again. Number 2361."

"Number 2361?" said Brigitte.

"In *The Ashley Book of Knots*," Lincoln explained, "which most of us just call *ABOK*. Ashley sorted out all the knots, hitches, bends, loops, everything by what they're used for, and gave each one a number. Plus instructions on how to tie them." Lincoln brushed a flop of hair back from his forehead and looked at them intensely, eyes shining. His face showed that he considered this a tremendous accomplishment. "Took him more than eleven years."

Paloma said, "Why?"

"Why give every knot a number? Much less confusion because a lot of knots have more than one name. And some knots are bad—wrong for certain jobs. *ABOK* explains everything."

Everyone stared at Lincoln. Paloma nudged Lucky with her foot and widened her eyes: *You didn't mention that he was so . . . unusual.* Lucky gave a slight shrug in response: *What can I tell you? Lincoln is Lincoln.* Mrs. Wellborne said, "Could you show me number 2361?" and held out the two ends of her scarf. Lincoln tied them in a loose knot that seemed easy but would be difficult, Lucky supposed, to remember later. Tied that way, the scarf looked quite elegant.

Lincoln and Mrs. Wellborne smiled at each other. This was not going the way Lucky had imagined. Shy, untalkative Lincoln seemed to have been taken over by an alien. "So is that rope in your bag? Are you making something?" Mrs. Wellborne asked him.

Lucky waited to see if Lincoln would tell the secret of what he was making for the contest. If it turned out to be a fishing net, she knew they would all realize how deeply weird he really was.

"Lincoln's mother thinks he's going to be the president of the United States when he grows up," Lucky said quickly. Lincoln hated to explain why his mother had named him Lincoln Clinton Carter Kennedy.

"Well, anything's possible in America," said Mrs. Wellborne. "Don't you think so, Brigitte?"

Brigitte laughed. "I tell you a little story about why I love to live here. When I first arrive in California, I see the sign on the highway, 'Soft Shoulder.' I think this is a very beautiful thing for a road sign to say: 'soft shoulder.'"

Mrs. Wellborne laughed and nodded.

"We do not have any like it in France, and I am curious. Later I learn it means the side of the road is too sandy and your car can get stuck. So 'soft shoulder' is a practical warning, but sweet. Like a small poem. It is a romantic way to see the world, just like to believe anything is possible." She shrugged. "Before, when I live in France, I believe *not* everything is possible. Never do I imagine that one day I will go to a little town in the middle of this big California desert or that, even working very hard, I can start my own business."

Lucky listened with some amazement. Usually Brigitte didn't share those kinds of private thoughts with someone she'd just met. The two moms must have really bonded because of those phone calls.

"And," Brigitte continued, "certainly never do I dream that the girl waiting inside a water tank house will later be my daughter. So now that I am almost American, I see out of my almost-American eyes that it is true: Anything *can* be possible. And if Lincoln does become president, he will be a very great one."

19. a pretty sweet deal

Well, thought Lucky, seeing Lincoln's ear tips turn pink, that finally shut *him* up. At the same time, "soft shoulder" gave her cheek a sudden strong longing to rub itself against her first mother's smooth, cool shoulder. Thinking about this made Lucky's heart feel tender and sore for a moment, like when you poke a deep bruise that is still healing. Then a slender arm encircled her, Brigitte's hand strong and firm on Lucky's own shoulder.

"But that boy who lied when you were little, why didn't you just bite *his* earlobes?" Miles asked. Everyone but Lucky, Lincoln, and Mrs. Wellborne looked puzzled. Lucky held her breath.

Mrs. Wellborne laughed again, throwing her head back and showing perfect, white, even teeth. "I miss that age," she said to Brigitte. "When they come up with such off-the-wall remarks." She winked at Miles.

Relief poured through Lucky's arteries like a flash flood. "Hey, Miles," she said, to keep him from pursuing this question, which she knew he would otherwise do. "How is *Brain Surgery for Beginners*?"

Miles eagerly pulled the book out of its Buy-Mor-Store plastic bag. He sat on the bag to keep it from blowing away. "This is the best book I ever read, so far," he said. "Lincoln and Lucky are helping me with the hard words. I found out that you can poke or squeeze a brain—it's true, it says so in the book—and it won't feel a thing. The brain," he explained, "depends on the skin to feel things."

Lucky noticed out of the corner of her eye that Paloma was about to go on a laughing jag again, so she closed her eyes, hoping for something to happen that would get the Wellbornes back in their Hummer, Lincoln and Miles back to their own houses, and herself and Paloma to the privacy of her canned-ham trailer.

Lucky said the first thing that popped into her mind. "Miles has been diagnosed as a genius."

"Diagnosed is the wrong word," Miles said, frowning. "That's for a disease."

"A genius!" Mrs. Wellborne said. "How nice! Your mother must be very proud of you."

"Well, she *would* be," Miles said, "but she's in j—"

"Look!" Lucky interrupted, before Miles could explain that his mother was in jail. Mr. Wellborne was tearing out of the kitchen trailer. "Mr. Wellborne is in a really big hurry!"

Jangling his keys as he started toward them, Mr. Wellborne said, "Brigitte, Lucky, appreciate the hospitality. Carmen, we have to get to a land line, right now, the one at the hotel in Sierra City. I got calls coming in, my lawyer and a couple producers in Honolulu. Lining up a pretty sweet deal." He turned to Paloma. "Baby, have fun," he said, and kissed the tip of her nose. Mr. Wellborne, who had Paloma's curly black eyelashes and droopy eyes, now looked much happier than when he'd arrived. Lucky smiled at Paloma sideways, so anyone paying attention would have thought she was smiling at Mr. Wellborne for lining up a pretty sweet deal. Paloma smiled sideways back at her.

"But—," Miles began.

"Miles," interrupted Lucky, standing up. "What time is the party on Sunday?" She already knew, but asked in order to distract him.

"Oh, yeah!" Miles said. "It's at four o'clock. You can come to our birthday party," he added to the Wellbornes. "Everyone in Hard Pan is coming, and it's at Short Sammy's water tank house because I'll be six and the next day Lucky'll be eleven. But we have a rule," he said seriously to Mrs. Wellborne, "that there is no earlobe-biting allowed. You have to be nice to boys."

Mrs. Wellborne laughed. "Absolutely," she said. Miles agreed happily when she told him she wanted to hear more about brain surgery later. "Brigitte, thank you and *merci beaucoup*, excuse my accent. The party sounds fun—we'll come if it's really okay. Then we'll see you at around four o'clock on

Sunday." She hugged Paloma. "Be good, sweetie. Don't forget your repellant and sunscreen and try to keep out of the sun. Don't wander off or go anywhere without letting Brigitte know where you are. And please, Paloma, remember to use good judgment!" Turning to Lucky, she added, "I know you'll be a fine influence, Lucky dear. You seem so mature for your age."

"Carmen," said Mr. Wellborne. "Gotta go."

"Okay! Don't worry!" Paloma called as her parents hurried to the Hummer.

Lincoln jumped up suddenly. "Mr. Wellborne, your cell!" he said, and strode to the car with it, and then held Mrs. Wellborne's purse while Mr. Wellborne helped her climb up the high step into the Hummer. Lucky ground her teeth. *Go*, she thought.

Lincoln said, "What's the ground clearance?"

"Sixteen inches," Mr. Wellborne answered. "Clears most terrain. Of course the H1 Alpha can ford thirty inches of water—it's got a central venting system to protect the drivetrain."

Lucky didn't have the faintest idea what this meant.

"Man," said Lincoln admiringly. "Five-speed?"

Mr. Wellborne nodded. Suddenly he wasn't in such a hurry. "Plus tow mode."

"Well," Lucky called loudly. "Bye! Hope your sweet deal works out!"

Brigitte frowned at her. When Lucky was only being polite!

"Best part is the agility," Mr. Wellborne went on, as if he

were a car salesman and not someone with calls waiting in Sierra City. "Would you believe an approach angle of seventy-two degrees?"

Lincoln smiled and shook his head. "Like climbing a wall, almost," he said.

"Scale a sixty percent slope," Mr. Wellborne added.

"Conference call?" said Mrs. Wellborne, winking at Lincoln.

"Right." Mr. Wellborne walked around to the driver's side. "I'll take you out in it one of these days," he told Lincoln. "Show you how it handles."

Lincoln grinned. "I'll be here," he said.

The Wellbornes waved, and then the tinted windows slid up and the huge vehicle took off, leaving behind a brown trail of road dust and the smell of diesel. Lucky sighed, thinking how strange it was that both Miles and Lincoln, *of all people*, had made a fabulous impression on the Wellbornes. The world can be a very mysterious place.

20. trouble

Finding out the exact (or almost exact) location of the Lost Brooch Well had been a lot easier than Lucky imagined.

She had simply asked the Captain straight out, when she ran into him outside the post office, figuring he would answer in that direct, thorough way of his, as if she were an adult. She was right: He picked up a stick and made a big angular arm shape in the gravelly sand. "Okay, here's California," he said, and she laughed. Then he drew the low hills that marked the northern boundary of Hard Pan, little upside-down V's, his house with its observation tower, and the post office. "You are here," he said, making an X.

He dragged the stick to show the direction to the well. There were abandoned miners' dug-outs and mines to mark the way. "You can do it in five minutes in a dune buggy," he said, which showed that he didn't suspect Lucky herself was planning to go there, even though that meant it was about a thirty-minute walk. He didn't even ask why she wanted to know, or warn her not to fool around at the well, or give her any advice. For an adult, the Captain was a very refreshing person.

Of course she'd worried about the problem of Lincoln and Miles wanting to tag along. But Miles, fortunately, was preoccupied with plans all over town for the party, and Dot was using Lincoln's knot-tying skills to "festivate" Short Sammy's water tank house with decorations.

Lucky and Paloma had helped with the lunch crowd at the Café on Saturday, and in the afternoon they'd hung out at the museum, checked out the broken-down cart at Dot's, and finished their homework. And since Monday was Lucky's birthday, Brigitte gave her Sunday off. She hired Sandi—who had worked as a waitress before she became the school bus driver—to help at the Café. The wonderful coincidence of this, getting a bus driver to bus tables, struck Lucky as a good omen. And she had been filled with gratitude that in spite of Brigitte's many flaws, such as being too French and acting weird about burros, she had understood the supreme importance of allowing Lucky a whole day to spend with Paloma.

Sunday morning, curled in her sleeping bag on the floor, Lucky woke and craned her neck around; she looked up into Paloma's deep blue eyes peering down at her from the bed. "You know," Paloma said, as if they were in the middle of a conversation, "tomorrow's your real birthday, which, I won't be here, so I'm declaring today 'Lucky's Birthday Observed.'"

Lucky grinned and flopped over onto her back. *This* is what having a best girlfriend was about.

"And here is your present from me, which, it's so you won't get lost in the desert."

It was a small brass compass with a hinged lid. It looked brand-new but very elegant and old-fashioned. Lucky slowly rotated the compass until the *N* was in line with the sensitive, trembling needle. "Wow, Paloma, I bet Charles Darwin had one just like this!"

Paloma looked pleased and said, "Well, I wasn't sure, which, my dad thought you'd rather have a GPS."

Lucky thought of *her* father, who never observed her birthdays at all. As usual, this made a needle of longing swing around and point straight at her heart; it was a longing to understand why he did not love her. She held the cool metal of the compass to her check and sniffed the new-brass smell. "No," she said to Paloma. "This compass is another way that Charles Darwin and I are alike. I'll never get lost because of you. And it is so cool that you were right and your dad was wrong. My father," she added—she never thought of him as "Dad"—"is wrong a lot." Then she didn't want to explain, so she jumped up and opened the portal windows, and sunlight streamed in along with a little breeze that made them both want to be outside.

They were starving. Lucky scrambled eggs with tomatoes and rolled them into warm corn tortillas, which they scarfed down at a Café table. Brigitte, still in her T-shirt nightgown and bare feet, brought orange juice along with a kiss for both cheeks of each girl. In France, Lucky knew, you are supposed to kiss back, but she always found this too embarrassing so she just let herself be kissed and left it at that.

Lucky and Paloma's plans for the morning, decided upon in private the night before, were to hike down to the old cemetery to look at fancy headstones from when Hard Pan was a booming mining town; have a picnic lunch on the museum's shady patio; stay away from the Café so they wouldn't get roped into helping after all; stay away from Short Sammy's, ditto; and, later, to do something intrepid.

So after the picnic, when Lucky was pretty sure there would be no remaining customers at the Café, they headed back home to round up supplies for their next adventure. They passed an old, dusty, dented Camry heading the other way. It was Sandi, apparently finished with busing tables at the Café. Lucky found it extremely strange to see her in anything other than the school bus, where, back when Lucky was in kindergarten, she believed that Sandi lived her whole life.

Brigitte was in the kitchen trailer, and cupcake tins covered every surface. "You and Paloma should arrive to Short Sammy's early," she said as she spread frosting on row after row of cupcakes. With a small plastic spatula, she slapped the soft chocolate on each little cake in a quick, neat, professional way. "Do these look right?" she asked.

"Perfect," said Paloma.

"We should taste one to be sure," said Lucky. Paloma's lips came apart and her smile beamed out.

"Yes, I make a few extras in case of this," Brigitte said. She cut a cupcake in two and gave each girl a half, breaking a small piece off for herself.

"Yum," Paloma said, and slid her eyes sideways at Lucky. This made Lucky realize how funny the word "yum" can be in certain situations, such as right then. Lucky knew she could burst out laughing very, very easily over "yum" and "yummy," and she squeezed her eyes tight shut, swallowed, and without looking at Paloma, said, "Very yum."

Paloma snorted and choked a little to keep from laughing. Pretty soon, Lucky knew, they wouldn't be able to control how funny everything was.

Brigitte looked closely at Lucky, smiling and frowning at the same time. She smoothed Lucky's garden-hedge hair back from her forehead. "Remember what I tell you before, Lucky, about trouble. This is important."

"I know," said Lucky, slipping on her backpack. "I'll remember."

Brigitte turned to Paloma and stroked her cheek with the backs of her fingers. "And you, *petit oiseau*, you will help Lucky to stay away from trouble?" Brigitte called Paloma "little bird" because of her name meaning dove.

"Sure! Which, I hope my mom won't call, but if she does,

you can tell her I took my vitamins and I put on loads of sun-screen, okay?"

But the second Lucky and Paloma jumped the steps of the trailer and ran toward the dry wash, they had completely forgotten whatever it was that Brigitte had been talking about.

21. intrepid

Lucky and Paloma peered into the Lost Brooch Well, leaning on the old timbers that framed the waist-high opening. Two ancient wooden posts with notches cut in their tops extended up from the sides, and a heavy metal pole lay across them, resting in the notches. A very show-offy person, Lucky imagined, could do pull-ups on that metal pole—but if she lost her grip, she would fall straight to the bottom of the well and be smashed to smithereens. Lucky was not that type of person, show-offy, but she *was* adventurous and brave, and there is a difference. She was almost almost almost eleven, and she was intrepid.

HMS Beagle finished sniffing around and lay down in the crooked shade of a nearby Joshua tree.

They couldn't see the bottom of the well, only darkness. "Oh good," said Lucky. "There's a ladder." She was eager to get down there and look for the missing piece of the brooch.

"Yeah," said Paloma, but not in a way of someone agreeing

to a good thing. It was more a way of saying that a ladder wasn't really a good thing at all.

"I'll go first," said Lucky.

"You have a flashlight?"

"In my backpack." Lucky no longer carried a complete and thorough survival kit backpack everywhere, the way she used to before she was sure that Brigitte would stay in Hard Pan, but she had brought basic necessities of toilet paper, Pixy Stix, water, a flashlight, and of course her new compass.

Paloma leaned over the edge again. She frowned. "This gives me the jimjams," she said.

"The ladder's fastened to the side of the well. It won't move. What could happen, as long as we hold on to the ladder and go slow?"

"I don't know. It just looks really scary."

"But think of the glory when we find the other piece of Paloma's brooch," Lucky said. "*Your* brooch!" She imagined a photograph of herself and Paloma on the front page of the *Eastern Sierra Star News*, with a big headline saying:

**INTREPID GIRLS FIND BEAUTIFUL MURDERED
WOMAN'S FAMOUS LOST BROOCH!**

But Paloma was gazing at the canyons and gullies and hills all around them. There were no roads or trails, and no sight of the town. Flies buzzed, and a huge crow cruised overhead.

They could hear the *whomp, whomp, whomp* of its wings. An ancient abandoned car lay sunk in the sand a little distance off. Lucky could see that Paloma's intrepidness was turning a little shaky.

Paloma scrunched her mouth over on one side. She said, "Hey, Lucky, guess what. This idea is arsy-varsy, which, let's just *say* we went into the well and not really do it."

In fact, Lucky too was becoming hesitant. The well looked bottomless, as if it went all the way to the center of the Earth, and an ancient, moldy smell came wafting up. But her adventuresome DNA overcame her cautiousness DNA. You cannot go around being scared of everything if you're a true scientist.

"Listen," she said. "I'll climb down while you wait here. When I get to the bottom I'll shout up to you, and then you'll know it's safe and you can decide if you want to climb down too." Lucky looked into Paloma's droopy, worried eyes. "Or not. It's okay if you don't want to. I won't start looking for the wing until you decide." She was willing to give Paloma first dibs on actually finding the brooch, although she would be sure to tell the newspaper reporters that it was she, Lucky Trimble, who climbed down first on the ladder.

Paloma shook her head. "I don't want *you* to go down there either," she said. "It's too creepy. And no one knows where we are, *I* don't know where we are, and if we get in trouble it'll be *real bad* double trouble."

Lucky clicked her tongue. This was exactly the sort of

argument Lincoln would make, because it wasn't just about going into the well: There was also a built-in fear because they were alone out in the desert and no one knew where. "I promise nothing will happen," she said. "Think of all the people who went up and down that ladder when they dug the well. It's no big deal. Look." Lucky hoisted herself up backward to sit on the frame of the opening, then swiveled around and swung her legs over so they dangled into the well. It felt sort of like being perched on the edge of the Grand Canyon. Then she took a deep breath and got a good grip on the old wood ladder. She reached for a rung with one foot and then the other, found it, and hung there, facing the inner wall of the well. She was sure the hardest part was over.

The only thing she had to do, now that she was actually in the well, was ignore the little clench of scariness in her stomach when she looked down into the blackness. Standing on the ladder, grinning up at Paloma, she lowered herself carefully down one rung.

She let go with one hand long enough to give a thumbs-up to Paloma when she had gone down another two rungs. It was up to her to show how fun and easy it was to be daring.

"Be careful," Paloma said. "Jeez. Hold on to the ladder."

Lucky could see that she was clutching the wooden beam at the top of the well so hard her fingertips were white.

"I am, don't worry. This is like going down stairs. Even *Miles* could practically do it."

But actually the rungs were far apart, being sized for a grown man, and required more strength than Lucky had anticipated. She took it slowly, not hand over hand but one rung at a time, pausing each time before reaching down again. A fleeting worry about how hard it was going to be to haul herself back *up* the ladder flashed into her mind, but she ignored it. She kept a good, firm grip on the splintery rungs, concentrating on each movement as she descended. It became cooler and darker, and once when she looked up she saw that Paloma's head had become a small dot against the blue of the sky.

After a few moments, Paloma called down, "I can't see you anymore, Lucky. You better come back up now."

"I'm sure I'm almost to the bottom," Lucky answered, her voice echoey. She hoped she was right, because she could not see much in the gloom, and certainly not the bottom of the well. How deep *was* the well, anyway? It seemed she'd been going down and down for a long time.

A tremendous surge gripped Lucky, of needing to finally reach her foot down and touch solid ground, to be done with climbing, to be able to rest. The muscles in her arms and legs trembled from the strain of supporting her body. She began, for the first time, to think this was a mistake.

Then two bad surprises occurred, and resulted in a third very bad thing, which caused Lucky to make a yowl that flew wildly up to the top of the well and straight into Paloma's terrified ears.

22. nothing's going to happen

What happened was this: As she was reaching down to the next rung, a splinter of wood pierced the palm of Lucky's hand. At the same time her right foot found a lower rung, and that rung snapped. Yowling, Lucky lost her grip and fell.

She had the wind knocked out of her from the suddenness of the fall, from the hard, painful slap to the bottoms of her feet as she landed, and from the sharp jab of the flashlight in her ribs when she lurched over onto her backpack. The floor of the well was damp, the smell thick and moldy.

"Lucky?" Paloma's voice sounded high and thin, the voice of someone who was about to cry.

It took a minute for Lucky to get her breath. Then she yelled, "Paloma! I made it! Well, I kind of made it!"

Lucky was shaking all over, and her hand felt like a hot needle had been driven inside it. She scrounged around in the backpack for her flashlight. Its beam was dim, the batteries very low. She got to her feet and shone the light on the broken ladder rung, which turned out to be the very bottom one. It was above her head and higher than her reach.

Paloma called, "What was that noise? Are you okay?"

"I got a splinter and I fell off the ladder. I can't stop shaking."

"HMS Beagle is acting very worried. She wants you to come up *now*."

Hey! Good idea! Why didn't I think of that? Lucky said to herself sarcastically. The bottom of the well was cold, cramped, dark, and musty, like some kind of cave where trolls would live. Suddenly she was tired of acting brave, weary of adventures, and sick of the well. Her brain corpuscles felt grouchy and snappish. "Well, fine!" she called. "I'll climb up as soon as I can figure out how to reach the ladder!"

"Is there anything down there you could stand on to reach it?"

Lucky rested for a while, beaming her dim flashlight around. There was a lot of junk that people must have thrown in: cans, an old tire, a boot. She saw a metal rod like the ones mechanics use to measure oil, and poked it through the trash.

Nothing solid enough to stand on and reach the ladder, not enough stuff to pile up to make a stool. Besides, she didn't think she had the strength to pull herself up to the unbroken rung.

Lucky looked up at the little patch of sky and the tiny head of Paloma. "Listen," she called. "I'm trapped in here. You're going to have to go get Short Sammy. Tell him not to tell Brigitte," she added.

"Okay." After a pause, Paloma said, "Which way?"

Lucky's flashlight got dimmer and dimmer and then went out altogether. Lucky ground the heel of her good hand into her forehead. "The way we came! Go back up that hill, over the crest, and you'll see Hard Pan on the other side." Lucky gestured toward Hard Pan, but Paloma, of course, couldn't see her.

"There are hills all around here, Lucky. I can't remember which one we came from."

"It's toward the southwest." Silence from above. "Paloma?"

"I don't know which way is southwest," Paloma admitted.

Lucky gripped the smooth round compass in her pocket. Useless! "BEAG," she shouted. "Go get Sammy! Go!"

"She hears you and she's sniffing all around the well," Paloma said. "But she's not going anywhere. Now she's lying down right next to the well."

"Look, Paloma, this isn't a TV show," Lucky said, even though sending her dog for help had been her own idea. "We need to get home before your parents arrive. Do you think you could *try* to find your way back? Because if you don't, we're stuck here until somebody happens to notice we're missing and they send out search parties. And that won't be until tonight, because of all the fuss about the party. And then we'll really be in trouble. You *have* to go."

"What if I get lost? You're not supposed to go wandering around in the desert alone."

"I know, they always tell you that, and I wish there was some way I could give you the compass. But nothing's going to happen." Lucky heard the echo of herself saying these very words before she climbed down the ladder, before something actually did happen. "Just remember to look back every so often and keep the well in sight. It's not that far. You'll be fine."

After a few minutes, Paloma leaned her head over the edge and said, "You're right. I'm going for help. I just want you to know that if . . . it doesn't work out, I don't blame you. You're the best friend I ever had. Good-bye, Lucky."

"Me too! Plus, you are the bravest! Tell Short Sammy to hurry!" Lucky wanted to get out of there, and the faster the better. She *hated* being in the well. "Go as fast as you can, okay?" Lucky craned her neck back again to see Paloma, but when she looked there was only the sky, bisected by the metal pole.

She frowned. She thought about Paloma trudging along in the sand. Paloma, who had absolutely no idea of direction. Paloma, who had hardly ever been to the desert before, never mind in the backcountry where there were no roads or trails. Who didn't know to make a triangle shape out of old tin cans as a signal that you needed to be rescued, or how to do SOS with a flashlight. Lucky began to realize that she had made a mistake in sending Paloma to get help. Maybe a very, very bad mistake.

There was still, probably, time to call out, to tell Paloma to stay put and wait. Lucky knew this would be the right thing to do. And she almost did call out. But then a gland she never knew existed started pumping thoughts about her own poor trapped self, and these thoughts grew so big, so important, that they grabbed Lucky's vocal cords and held them tightly closed. So after a while, when Lucky finally did call out, when she shouted and screamed as loud as she could, there was no answer, no head of Paloma peering down at her.

It was too late.

23. alone

Where, Lucky wondered, are the geologists when you need them? Where are the sedimentologists, the paleontologists, the seismologists, and the mineralogists? Why weren't they out looking at rocks and discovering the mess Lucky was in? Where was Dot, the Captain, Short Sammy, and Mrs. Prender? Where, especially, was Brigitte? Why were they all too busy to notice that she was in trouble and needed them?

Where was Lincoln?????

The situation of being alone at the bottom of a well with no way to get herself out, and having no flashlight in the darkness, and nobody knowing where she was, and her best friend lost and wandering in the desert due to Lucky's stupidly *ordering* her to, and her oldest friend, Lincoln, hating her—he had to hate her for what she did to his net—the situation was the worst she could ever, ever imagine. It made Lucky as sad as if the world had completely ended and she was the only person left. Tears poured out of her eyes. Everything would be a little tiny bit better if only it were someone else's fault, but all of it, every speck of awfulness, was Lucky's exclusive fault, and she knew it.

Lucky cried miserably for a long while. She needed to blow her nose, and thinking of the toilet paper in the backpack reminded her of the Pixy Stix she'd brought in case of emergency. Pixy Stix comfort you when you are in a sad or desperate situation, and it is always good to have some on hand. They look like straws, but instead of being empty, the paper tubes are filled with very delicious grainy granules, like sugar but in different colors and flavors. You tear off either end of the straw and pour the grains onto your tongue. You can pour a lot to fill up your mouth, or a little, to make your Pixy Stix last a longer time.

But a strange thing had happened, because her backpack was wet clear through. Lucky felt around inside and found the reason. The cap of the plastic water bottle had been knocked loose—probably when she fell. So the toilet paper roll was wet and useless, and the Pixy Stix in their paper straws were rock solid and soaked. Lucky tried to slit the paper of the straw in order to salvage the candy, which could no longer be poured but perhaps could be scraped off with her teeth. But her arm muscles were still getting over the strain of climbing down, they were weak and noodle-y, and she dropped all five Pixy Stix on the ground. She would not pick them up—it was too yucky and too dark to see what muck from the ground was on them. Lucky put her head down on her knees and sobbed. No water, no toilet paper, and *even her Pixy Stix were ruined*!

24. a mummy

After a time, Lucky discovered that being bored is actually almost worse than being sad. When you are sad, your heart pumps the tragedy all through your body and fills your mind with the story of your suffering, and you tell that story to your-self over and over. But when you are bored, your mind has no stories and is a gray lump, a lump with soggy crevices of longing for something to happen. Bored is bad; bored and all alone in the universe is dreadful; but bored and all alone in the universe and hungry and thirsty and sad in the dark is . . . Lucky searched for the right word. *It's like death*, she thought. *Death would even be* better *than this*.

If she were to die in the well, of starvation/sadness/boredom/thirst/loneliness, Lucky realized it might be so long before they finally found her that she would have become a mummy. This thought cheered her up quite a lot, because if she were a mummy she could be displayed in the Found

Object Wind Chime Museum and Visitor Center and become a big attraction, since it's not a common thing to see actual mummies. Even her father would come to see her mummified self—he would *have* to—and he would be proud and sorry. Proud of her magnificent courage; he would not realize how scared she'd been. And sorry because he had never known her before she died; it was too late now. And at last he would realize how wrong that had been.

Lucky knew that the very dry desert air was perfect for mummification, because she had once found a mouse mummy in an old abandoned shack. It was not all wrapped in cloth like ancient Egyptian mummies, which had become mummies because people had carefully removed their internal organs. Lucky had read, and she believed it to be true, that the ancient Egyptians removed the brain of the dead person by sticking little instruments, little teeny spoons with long handles, up inside the head through the nostrils and *scooping* the brain out! Bit by bit!

But if the mouse mummy was reliable proof, which Lucky thought it probably must be, then other animals around Hard Pan could be wonderfully preserved as natural mummies too, because all the fluids and internal organs would dry up. The air would suck out every speck of moisture so nothing was left to decay, just skin and bones and fur would be all that was left.

The mouse had been on its side at the time of death, and its mummy was flat as a pancake. Lucky thought that just before she died she ought to remember to lie in a nice, attractive position. It was frustrating that the terrible well was too cramped for this. She would have preferred to be an elegant mummy, languid and serene.

Thinking of her position, and her mummification and display in the Found Object Wind Chime Museum and Visitor Center, Lucky wished she had some light and a pencil and paper in order to write a good description for the display case. Something like, "Genuine Mummy of Intrepid Young Explorer Who Died Heroically When Trapped in Lost Brooch Well." Lucky considered. She hadn't really done anything heroic yet. How frustrating! She wracked her brain for a heroic deed, even something from a long time ago, but couldn't think of any.

130

Lucky was about to make *up* a heroic deed or two when she felt something brush her cheek. It felt sticky-cobwebby, and a new terrible thought of black widow spiders crept into her brain: Since they like living in caves, as Lucky knew from Miles's grandmother, then they must *love* old abandoned wells. If there were black widows in the well and Lucky was bothering them in their work of catching things in their webs, and if they stung her because they thought she would take their bug-victims and eat them herself, then she was in truly big trouble.

Lucky was pretty sure that nothing hurt worse than a black widow spider bite. It makes your skin die. It sends poison through your body and causes horrible cramps and throwing up. If you're at home, you go right away to the hospital, but if you're in a well in the desert and can't get out, you will probably die a wretched long lonely death, wrapped in pain.

Lucky stayed very still to show the spiders that she wasn't there to steal their dinner or disturb their webs. She wanted them to know that she hadn't meant to invade their home. *Please don't bite me. I'm not good to eat,* she thought at them. *I'm too big. And I won't hurt you, and I won't steal your bugs, and I didn't mean to disturb you. So please don't bite me, please please please don't bite me.* But she didn't know if spiders could understand thought-waves, even urgent, desperate thought-waves, so she sat still and breathed and remembered.

Lucky remembered a time when she was seven years old. *Just breathe,* her first mother Lucille would whisper when they sat together on the big Thinking Chair. This was in the time before Lucille died. Lucille was a painter, and sometimes she would sit in her big chair, concentrating and staring at a blank page in her Arches pad of thick, thick watercolor paper. Lucky understood that when Lucille sat in her chair and stared at her paper it wasn't a time for talking, so she perched on the wide green arm of the chair and rubbed her cheek against Lucille's soft round shoulder, and breathed the Lucille-smells of paint and paint thinner. When her mother was almost ready to begin painting, she would hum or sing. "*Que sera, sera,* whatever will be, will be," were the words Lucky remembered now, for it seemed to be a song about Lucky's very situation, a song about the future, and how whatever happens, happens.

After her mother died, when Lucky was sad or missing Lucille, she would sit on the green arm of the chair in her mind, breathing with her mother. And now, in the well, Lucky calmed herself by thinking whatever will be, will be, for there was nothing she could do, not one thing, to save herself. After shouting and crying and raging and imagining herself a mummy and wishing she were heroic and thinking at spiders and missing her mom, Lucky was worn down. Finally, not caring any longer, she let her head fall upon her knees and gave up.

Then, although she was as alone as she'd ever been in her life, Lucky heard, inside her head, first the sharp click of Brigitte's tongue, and then her deep voice. "*Ah, non, ma puce,*" said the voice inside Lucky's brain. It was Brigitte's bristling-mad voice.

"The future does not happen just by chance."

Lucky moaned, because she did not want to talk to Brigitte in her mind about the future.

"And now, you give up? I am disappointed, Lucky. Your first *maman* raised you to be brave, and always I see that you are a fighter."

I'm not lucky, Lucky thought miserably. *I ran out of luck. There's nothing more I can do.*

"You are eleven years old tomorrow! How can you dare to give up?"

And Lucky had an eleven-ish thought, a new thought that burned her with shame. If she died, right on the tip of ten, right on the brink of eleven, it would be her own fault. People would talk about how they'd always thought she was a sensible person, but climbing down into an abandoned well? Going out in the desert without letting anyone know? Endangering her new friend? The idea of this was too dreadful and embarrassing to bear. She jumped up, backing away from where she thought the black widow web was. Cupping her hands around her mouth to make a megaphone, she shouted with all her might. "Hey! Down here! In the well! Help!"

And pausing to gulp air, Lucky heard a far-off voice, Lincoln's voice, saying, "I hear her! Over there!"

25. a dangerous world

"Lucky?" It was Paloma, her head tiny at the opening above.

"Paloma!" Lucky felt a huge surge of relief. Paloma hadn't gotten lost, and she, Lucky, had been found.

"Lincoln," Paloma said, "you were right! This is the well! I thought it was way over by that foothill!"

Then Lincoln laughed. Laughed!

Like this was a little picnic! Fine for them, with no splinters like hot needles in their hands, and with all the Pixy Stix they wanted, but what about her? They should have been *gravely* concerned about whether she was even, after all these hours and hours, still alive! Plus, *plus* the fact that Paloma evidently hadn't followed her specific instructions to get Short Sammy.

Maybe it had slipped their minds that she was almost a complete *mummy*, in the bottom of some totally dark *well*, with a splinter that was probably an inch long, no food or drink for *hours*; yes, they must have just forgotten all about her, because *they were laughing.* Lucky heel-kicked the wooden wall of the well. Her throat and cheeks burned; the roots of her hair sizzled. The shocked and angry molecules coursing through her body almost gave her the power to spring high enough to reach the ladder, surge up it like Spiderman, and leap out and crack their two heads together with all her might.

"Hey!" she called. "This isn't funny down here!"

"Hi, Lucky," said Lincoln. "We were just laughing at Paloma's sense of direction. Are you okay?" His head appeared at the rim of the well beside Paloma's.

"Lincoln, would you please go get Short Sammy, which is what I *thought* Paloma was supposed to do, so I can get out of here?"

"Hey, Lucky!" Paloma called in a cheerful voice, ignoring Lucky's sarcasm. "Guess what! I met Lincoln on his way here, so we made it back in only twenty minutes!"

Lucky knew positively that she'd been in the well for hours, but she held back this retort. She wasn't in a position to start an argument.

"Oh, *fine*," she called up. "That's *great*. How do you think you're going to get me out of here, Lincoln? You have no idea what it's like from where I'm standing. Even if you climb down, you'd never be able to climb back up; it's too hard. The ladder rungs are too far apart. It will have to be a strong grown-up who can piggyback me out. I really wish people would listen to what I *originally* said and get Short Sammy or the Captain. And Lincoln—"

"Hang on, Lucky," Lincoln called down in his calm, take-it-easy voice. "We'll have you out of there in a few minutes. You sound okay, but do you need anything? Water?"

"Yeah, drop a bottle down that will give me a brain concussion when it lands on my head. Then, oh yeah, I know what: Send Miles down so he can do a little brain surgery on me."

More laughter. Then Lincoln, saying, "I'd like to find out how deep the well is. Let me know when the bottle gets to the bottom." And Lucky saw something swaying at the opening, slowly being lowered, bumping the sides of the well on its way down. A bottle of water on a rope.

The clear plastic glinted enough in the light from above for Lucky to see it as it reached her. Lincoln's calmness and his lack of one speck of sympathy for her dreadful plight made Lucky reach out and jerk the bottle as hard as she could. The rope immediately fell on her in a heap, as Lincoln said, "Hey!"

"Wow," Paloma said after a second. "She jerked it right out of your hands!"

Lucky felt tears begin to pour out of her eyes again. They were discussing her as if *she* were the problem, instead of them not getting Short Sammy or someone right *now* to rescue her. She pressed the heels of her hands hard against her eye sockets to make herself stop crying. "Lincoln!" she shouted. "Never mind about me, but you might want to think about the fact that we'll all be in big trouble if we don't get back to Hard Pan pretty soon!"

Mumbled talk from above, then Lincoln's voice. "Working on it, Lucky. Patience."

Lucky couldn't stand not knowing what was going on. "Hey, Paloma," she yelled. "Why didn't you bring Short Sammy like I told you?"

But it was Lincoln who answered. "He's got something going on, pretty serious, but we're not sure what it's about." Lincoln interrupted himself to say something to Paloma that Lucky couldn't hear. Then he continued, "He came back from working on his adopted highway two hours ago and went straight into his house and closed the door. So I finished up decorating with Dot and thought I'd see what was happening out here—I figured you'd be here. Found Paloma heading toward Death Valley."

Paloma had been way off course, Lucky realized. If Lincoln hadn't come along, she'd be lost by now for sure. Lucky didn't want to think about that.

"The thing with Short Sammy—what's going on? Is it something to do with that box?"

But no one answered, and Lucky's neck hurt from craning up at the opening way above. She hunkered down and took a swig from Lincoln's bottle, thinking how sad and dangerous the world was when you least expected it, with people losing their way and buying coffins and closing their door so you didn't even know what was wrong.

If only she could trade this stinking black hole for the strong bright light on the surface, and trade the grip of the earth holding her below for Brigitte's encircling arms. Lucky waited, and she despaired.

26. an old tire rim

She heard Lincoln fooling around for a long time, talking in a low voice to Paloma, once getting HMS Beagle to go lie somewhere else. Time was a thick, murky soup in which Lucky was submerged.

Finally she couldn't bear it any longer. "Hey," she called. "What's going on? What're you doing?"

"Listen," Lincoln said after a minute. "I'm sending down some rope. This time it's secured up here, but don't jerk it, and let me know when it gets to where you can grasp it easily."

"Lincoln, my hand is badly hurt!" Lucky pressed a finger against her palm until she located the splinter, which was no longer painful but which *could* get infected or might already *be* infected. She imagined herself being hauled up by a rope around her waist. She did not like this idea. "I can't use my hand, and I'll never be able to tie a rope around myself."

"And I'd never let you; you wouldn't know the right knots," Lincoln said. "I'm making a pulley. Please let us handle this."

"A *pulley*?" Lucky retorted, as if he had said a "washing machine" or a "vacuum cleaner." "What kind of ridiculous plan do you have? If you drop me, you'll break *every bone in my body*."

There was no answer to this, but Lucky could hear them talking quietly to each other, most of the words indistinct but probably to result in her horrible death. Then clearly, there was Lincoln saying,". . . and see if you can yank out that tire rim by the old car."

"Lincoln!" Lucky shouted. "Forget the tire rim! Whatever your plan is, don't do it! Go get someone *now* who can rescue me from becoming a mummy or a pile of broken bones!"

Suddenly Lucky heard metal clanging on metal.

"It worked! Catch this end when I throw it over the top." Lincoln was now talking to Paloma, apparently. "See if you can bring it around to me—wait; go under the post. Yeah, perfect; got it. I have to test the weight. The knots and the rope are fine, but I'm not sure about these old posts and the pole."

"What's happening?" Lucky demanded.

No one answered. Lincoln said, not to her, "This is my safety. If the pole or the posts don't hold, my line's attached to the ladder. We'll have to trust it."

"This is scaring me to death," Paloma said. "Which, what if the ladder doesn't hold? You'll fall all the way and kill both of you."

"It's the third safety and I did test it; it'll hold. But *if* you have to go for help, you know the way now?"

"Wait!" yelled Lucky. "What are you *doing*?"

Lincoln's head appeared at the rim above.

"You'll be up here in another ten minutes, if you relax and cooperate."

"No! I won't! It's impossible, and what does an old tire rim have to do with this?"

"Lucky," Lincoln said, in a warning kind of way that was not at all like his usual, calm, knot-tying tone. It was a voice in control of the situation, a voice that knew what it was doing and had had enough of explanations. "Just. Shut. Up." After a moment, this being Lincoln, he added, "Please." And even though she had many questions, suggestions, and orders that badly needed to be communicated, Lucky did.

But now part of her couldn't wait for Lincoln's stupid plan to fail, so she would be right, and he would be wrong.

27. lincoln's net

Lucky saw the opening of the well fill up with arms and legs, which blotted out the sky. "Try pulling that end, Paloma," Lincoln instructed. "See if you can handle my weight . . . good. Keep it taut around the pole. Okay. It'll work." Then Lincoln pulled himself out again.

"Heads up!" Lincoln called down at her. Lucky saw that some large, floppy thing was descending. "Shout out when it's about a foot off the ground."

"Are you talking to me?" demanded Lucky. She did not like that everyone knew what was going on but her. She did not like being given orders. She did not like not being consulted. And she definitely did not like being the rescuee instead of the rescuer.

"And try not to get it all tangled up!" Lincoln cautioned.

By the time the thing was level with her head and Lucky touched it, she knew it was that big net Lincoln had been working on for so long. His fishing net from the black plastic trash bag.

The net that she had cut with scissors in three separate places.

Obviously, she was supposed to get into the net and be hauled up.

"No!" Lucky shouted. "I'm not some fish, and I'm not getting into your net! It'll break or you'll drop me!" She heard Paloma laughing. Paloma was only supposed to laugh *with* Lucky. Not *at* Lucky. "And quit laughing, Paloma!" she added.

"She's not laughing at you," Lincoln said impatiently. "Pay attention, Lucky. Is it low enough?" he called. "Should I stop lowering?"

"Almost . . . Okay, stop. It's a foot off the floor. But don't expect me to get into that fish net."

"It's a hammock, Lucky," Lincoln said. "Sit on it with your legs hanging down, and hold on to each side, like on a swing at the playground. Tell me when you're ready. And don't worry. We won't drop you."

Lucky considered refusing to get into the hammock—what a stupid project, anyway, a hammock, since Lincoln was no *way* the type to take naps; and what if the tear-repairs didn't hold?—but she decided, instead, to be intrepid. Maybe this would turn out to be the heroic act, the last she would ever do: the act of trusting Lincoln.

The hammock was a net made with smooth, thin cords in an open weave. Two long ropes extended from the ends of the swaying net up to the top of the well, where they joined into one single rope. She found her wet backpack, the dead flashlight, the water-bottle rope she'd jerked out of Lincoln's hands. Suddenly she realized that she hadn't even tried to find the fragment of the lost brooch. But she was done with the well, and the brooch, forever.

She steadied the hammock and backed into it, bunching up the netting at each side to give herself a good, firm grip. She sat, testing her weight, and took a deep breath. "Okay, I'm ready," she called.

And then slowly, slowly, the hammock swing began to rise, with brief stops at intervals as Lucky dangled. Lincoln's voice became clearer, orchestrating some kind of system with Paloma where they pulled, anchored the rope so it couldn't slip, pulled, anchored. With the useless soggy former survival kit on her back, Lucky rode up to the surface in Lincoln's net, heading for the light.

28. two-strand knots

There was one tricky part, at the very top, where she had to
kind of take a flying leap, with Paloma pushing the net-swing
from behind and Lincoln waiting to catch her as she sailed out
over the edge of the well, but it worked and Lucky was free.
HMS Beagle crowded in close, sniffing, and Lucky hugged her
until she stopped feeling shaky.

For a person who is close to becoming a mummy one minute, and who then turns out to be completely alive with only
a little splinter and no other major damage ten minutes later,
the world is a little odd. Nobody else realizes what it's like to
wait alone at the bottom of a dark well. All they think about is
to hurry up and get home before the adults find out. A part of
Lucky *wanted* the adults to find out, so they would respect her
heroism and courage. But another part of her, a realistic part,
knew that she would only get into big trouble, and Paloma,
too. And still *another* part of Lucky thought her friends, at

least, should be congratulating her, and asking her all about what it had been like, and admiring her intrepidness. It was irritating that they didn't do this. So in return Lucky acted as if the rescue operation was equally no big deal. She slammed her heart shut, hugged her dog, and said nothing.

Her two friends were slapping palms together and carefully gathering the net, Paloma admiring the brilliance of Lincoln's improvised pulley made from the old tire rim. It wasn't that they ignored her, just that they were filled with their own victory and triumph: They were the glorious rescuers. Feeling left out, Lucky cradled her hand. She hoped it would get infected and leave a scar. "I've got to get this hand looked at," she said. "I think it's pretty serious." Even Lucky herself thought this sounded like bad TV.

"Let me see it," Paloma said, and examined the splinter at close range. "Well, I bet it hurts a little, but it's small and not deep. Which, I can get it out easily with a pair of tweezers. Remind me when we get back. My mom made me bring this complete first aid kit. Lincoln, let me carry the other rope."

Lincoln was looking at the well. "I should come back tomorrow with some boards and barbed wire," he said. "Nail it over that opening."

Lucky gathered all her dignity. "*I'll* do it," she said. "That stupid well should be *completely* off-limits. Imagine if some *child* was playing here and—"

Lucky stopped. Paloma had pulled her lips inside and

widened her eyes. Then she looked at Lincoln and pointed at Lucky and said, "'*Completely* off-limits!'" Lincoln grinned and said, "'Imagine if some *child* was playing around here!'" They howled with laughter and then Lincoln said, "You may be right about that, Lucky, now that I think of it." And he stuffed the net carefully back into his black plastic trash bag, slung it over his shoulder, and turned toward Hard Pan.

Then he looked back. He said, "It was a round turn, and two half hitches through the beckets at the ends of the hammock that did it. I wasn't worried about the strain; that net's got a lot of weight-bearing strength and I repaired all the tears—or actually, the cuts—with two-strand knots. So it was able to take a lot of stress."

His bringing up how she had cut his net like that, without straight-out accusing her, made embarrassment and shame surge up through Lucky's body to right under the skin of her face; they made it red and hot. A bad taste rose into her throat from deep down at the back of her stomach where bile was waiting. It was the bitter flavor, too strong to bear, of knowing you'd been wrong and acted mean, and Lucky tried to bury the wretched taste of it under more meanness. "Lincoln," she said, in an exasperated tone. "What about *my* stress? Can you even imagine what I've been through? And can we please talk about something besides knots?" She noticed Paloma off to the side, no longer laughing, staring at her.

Lincoln repositioned the sack over his shoulder, gripping

its neck with both hands. He gazed at Lucky for a moment, nodded, turned away, and strode off toward Hard Pan.

"Bye!" Lucky called in a light tone to show she didn't care; to show that she had Paloma and didn't need him anymore.

Paloma continued to look at Lucky, her droopy eyes stunned. Finally she said, "Lincoln's pulley contraption was so cool." They set off behind him. "Which, I bet we could have hauled up an elephant, just the two of us."

Lucky said nothing. She trudged on, sand filling her shoes like grains of misery. A crow screamed from far overhead.

"Want a Maui Punch?" Paloma offered her a blue Pixy Stix.

Lucky took it, ripped the top off the paper straw, tipped her head back, and poured every speck of Pixy onto her tongue. Usually she made her Pixy Stix last much longer, but this time she wanted everything at once. She wanted her whole mouth to close around that Maui Punch flavor, which Paloma had saved for her.

"Paloma," she said, "I . . . should never have sent you out, like, practically to your doom. You were almost lost."

"Lost—are you kidding? With *my* mother?" Paloma said. "No way I was going to get lost. I found a stick and dragged it along to mark the ground, which, if I had to retrace my steps I probably could have. Of course, I was going in the complete wrong direction, so if Lincoln hadn't seen me I would have come back. He was looking for you. The thing is—" Paloma broke off.

"What?"

"Well, the thing is, he likes you, Lucky. Which, I don't get why you're so mean to him."

Lucky shrugged. She already knew Lincoln liked her. She knew that *she* would never like someone like her. She would hate someone like her. She would really, really hate someone who acted like her, and she'd get as far away as she could. *But how,* Lucky thought, *do you get away from someone you can't stand if that person is you?*

149

Paloma said, "Anyway, I told him you needed Short Sammy and he asked what was going on, so I explained how you were trapped in the well. He said he could get you out, which, I told him you really wanted Sammy."

As they walked, Lucky asked, "What was the thing that happened with Short Sammy, anyway?"

"It was strange," Paloma said. "Lincoln explained more of it to me on our way back to the well. He said Short Sammy left the Captain in charge of stirring the stew while he went out to work on his adopted highway. He was supposed to be back in about an hour. Which, after two hours the Captain started to wonder. Sammy hadn't returned."

"Probably more trash on the highway than usual," Lucky said, "because it's the weekend."

"That's what everyone thought," Paloma said, carefully avoiding a prickly-looking bush. "But then Sammy came driving back in his Cadillac. He's so short, Lincoln said all you could see through the window was his hat. But it turned out he wasn't alone in the car."

"He found someone out on the highway who needed help?" Lucky asked.

"Kind of. He found a dog."

"What dog would be way out here on a highway in the middle of nowhere?"

"Lincoln didn't know. It's a mystery," said Paloma. "But Sammy had come home, and he got out of the car with the dog in his arms, went straight into his water tank house, and shut the door behind him. He wouldn't answer the door to anyone. So Lincoln and I came back to get you out ourselves."

"Wow," said Lucky. "That is so messed up." She was sure that Sammy would have come running if he'd known the grave danger she'd been in. Lucky's white blood cells pumped out resentment antibodies. She felt a little bit cheated, and mad at Sammy, and mad, weirdly, at Lincoln for being able to so easily do what a grown-up should have been in charge of, and mad at Paloma for being so cheerful about everything. And mad, most of all, at Lucky Trimble for not being able to stop herself from having all these stupid thoughts.

"Pal," she said. "Do you know that you're always saying 'which'?"

Paloma looked confused. "When?"

"Like, all the time. You'll say something and then you say something about what you just said."

"I do?"

"Yeah. It's like you'll say—this is just an example—'Lincoln always ties knots, which, how weenie is that?'"

"I'd never say that!"

"It was just an example."

"I mean, I'd never say weenie, which, it's such a baby word."

"See, you just did it—," Lucky began.

Paloma whirled around to stand in front of Lucky. To the side, a little waist-high group of prickly cholla, backlit by the sun, glowed as if wearing halos. "And I'd never call Lincoln anything bad. Which, I mean, Lucky, jeez. I'd still be wandering around in the desert and you'd be at the bottom of that abandoned well right now if it weren't for him. Would you please give him a break?"

Lucky flung her head all the way back as far as it would go and then flopped it all the way forward as a way of saying *Yes* and *Duh* and *That's really beside the point.* "I know that, Pal," she said patiently, as if explaining something to a young child. "All I meant is about how you say 'which' all the time."

"Okay! I'll say something without saying 'which.' You're *horrid* to Lincoln!"

Then Paloma, Lucky's Pal, turned and ran on ahead, finally catching up to Lincoln. With HMS Beagle waiting beside her, Lucky stood where she was, tasting not the leftover sweetness of Maui Punch but a bad, bitter mixture of regret and loss.

"Beag," she said finally. "I lost them." HMS Beagle glanced at her, then pointed her nose at the jumble of footprints left by Lincoln and Paloma. Lucky nodded. "I know, but I ruined everything." Her dog stood staring straight ahead. "We should go find them, shouldn't we?" Lucky said. "At least we should try." The Beag agreed, and they began walking toward home.

29. something happened to lucky

Lucky smelled the stew all the way from the top of the hill. It was a tender-meat-and-vegetable smell that made you want to grab a bowl and a spoon. But as soon as the water tank house came into view, Miles came crashing toward them, and HMS Beagle charged toward Miles. "Where *were* you?" demanded Miles, his arms full of dog. "I waited and waited for you! My mom called! She's coming home in April! Only seven months!"

153

Seeing Miles like this made Lucky understand the expression, "He was beside himself." It was like Miles was so excited his skin couldn't handle the job of keeping him contained inside it. He went on, "The party's starting, and Short Sammy won't come out of his house, and Brigitte brought the 'ologists, but it's okay because the Captain says there's enough stew for an *army*. Plus, I was *worried*, Lucky. You shouldn't make me worry so much like that, especially when it's our birthdays."

"I know," said Lucky, grateful that at least *Miles* had worried about her. "I shouldn't have been gone so long." His hair had been cut in a way that let you see the darker soft undercoat, a thick cushion for the coppery curls on top. His neck seemed very small and vulnerable. Lucky curled her hand gently around the back of that little-boy neck. "Happy birthday, Miles," she said.

Miles looked up and frowned at her. "Did something happen to you, Lucky?" he asked.

Lucky laughed the kind of laugh when it's not about something funny, and then said, "Let's just say I've had my ups and downs today, Miles."

"No one *ever* explains things to me," Miles complained. "Even though I'm a whole year older, I still don't understand anything."

"Don't worry, Miles," Lucky said, her voice now sad and resigned, like a grown-up's. "Neither do I."

"But guess what! We found out what Short Sammy's box had in it! A bathtub! The Captain explained it to us, because Sammy's in his house with the door closed."

"A bathtub? What would Sammy do with a bathtub?"

"Well, later, when he uses it *as* a bathtub, he told the Captain he'll soak under the stars and listen to the L.A. traffic report and have the best bathroom in the world—outside! He'll fill her up in the morning, cover the tub with a sheet of black plastic, and pretty soon the water will be heated by the sun. Plus, he can drain it to water his plants. And it's half-sunk in a hole, but resting on cinderblocks, so he can build a fire underneath the tub in winter—it's cast-iron. That's why it was so heavy."

Lucky was absorbing all this, and her heart squeezed and squeezed itself with relief that it was not a casket after all. "But what did you mean when you said, 'when he uses it as a bathtub'? What else would he use it for?"

"Can't you smell it? He and the Captain cooked a stew with fourteen chickens in it! And onions and carrots and potatoes and celery, Lucky. A big army-regulation birthday chicken stew."

"But—in a bathtub?"

"Come *on*, Lucky," Miles said, pulling her hand, pulling her toward the laughter and the celebration. "It's a real old tub," he explained as they walked, "but Short Sammy had the inside re-enameled by a buddy of his, so it's like a brand-new cooking pot. Brigitte took pictures and said it was the most amazing American thing she ever saw."

And at that moment, Brigitte herself came running toward them, wearing an apron and a worried scowl—a lot like the gaze that could pin you to your chair and see the bad thoughts hidden in your mind.

30. safe

"Miles," Brigitte said, pulling off her apron, "please take this to the Captain. Tell him I come back soon to help, after I talk with Lucky."

"Wait," Lucky said. "Take HMS Beagle with you and give her a bowl of water, okay? I'll be right there."

"Okay, but hurry!" Miles said, and, followed by the dog, he ran back to the party.

Brigitte sat on the ground and pulled Lucky down next to her. "Are you all right, Lucky? You smell funny, like inside a tomb. And I see that you were crying and you are covered with dirt. You have been doing what?" Brigitte held Lucky's face close to her own face, peering into her eyes as if Lucky were a precious fragile doll.

"Nothing. Just fooling around. I got a splinter."

Brigitte examined Lucky's palm, said that the splinter would come out easily, then looked again with her blue-green eyes into Lucky's light brown ones. Lucky tried to twist away but Brigitte held her face, waiting. Lucky tried to stare back, but it was like looking at the sun. It seared her eyeballs and made tears well up behind them. Calm and steady, Brigitte still waited.

"I climbed down into an abandoned well," Lucky said finally. "The ladder broke and Paloma went for help and she got lost but Lincoln found her and then they came and fished me out with his net."

"Oh, *ma puce*." Brigitte sighed and wrapped her arms tightly around Lucky.

"But now Lincoln hates me," Lucky said, beginning to cry. She felt as if she'd been laboring all day long: trudging around in the desert, crying hard, being mad, being scared. She felt deeply weary.

"Why does Lincoln rescue you if he hates you?" Brigitte asked.

"He'll always rescue people, even ones who are hateful."

"This is confusing, Lucky. You and Lincoln do not hate each other."

Lucky didn't answer. She shook her head against Brigitte's shoulder.

Brigitte said, "You are smart, *ma fille*, but not always sensible."

Lucky loved it when Brigitte called her "my daughter." "I know," she said, and she truly did.

After a while Lucky stopped crying and Brigitte said, "I hope Paloma does not have this smell of earth too. Her *maman* will not like it."

"No," Lucky said. "Paloma was smart *and* sensible. I should have listened to her."

"Mmmm. Good. I think the next time you will listen to Paloma if there is a question of danger. And maybe you will listen to your own big heart when there is a question about Lincoln. Now we go to the party and eat a very good dinner from a bathtub, and later tonight you will tell me more."

"Yes," said Lucky, and made to get up. But Brigitte said, "Wait," and pulled a small hinged box from her pocket. "It is very old," she said. "It first belongs to my *arrière-grand-mère*, the mother of the mother of my mother. My mother give it to me when I am eleven and now I give it to you for your birthday."

It was a sparkling deep red jewel, a ruby, Brigitte explained, in a gold setting on a thin gold chain. The necklace, light and delicate, had been worn for years and years, for *generations*, by Brigitte's relatives. Now Lucky realized that she herself was also connected, that the links of the chain reached across distance and time to encircle her with those relatives. She lifted her hair so that Brigitte could fasten the clasp at the back of her neck. She felt, suddenly, a little bit French. During all the time that Brigitte had been becoming more American, Lucky never once thought that she, too, might change. She traced the outline of the ruby against her skin and had a sensation of having evolved in some invisible way. She carefully stowed the box in a safe place in her backpack and kissed Brigitte on each cheek, exactly the way a French daughter would do.

Brigitte put her hands on Lucky's shoulders. "One more thing, Lucky. Since I am only a beginning parent, I am not sure of what will be your punishment. Maybe you can give me advice, when we talk. You will explain to me what other mothers will do when their daughters do not obey. When there is broken trust. What do you think, Lucky?"

Lucky knew Brigitte was both serious, the part about her punishment, and teasing, because of Lucky's frequent reminders that she was only a beginning parent. "Okay," she said.

And then suddenly Lucky had a question. "Brigitte, why does my father hate me?"

Brigitte scowled. "It is true that he behaves very badly, horribly; he is not a father to you at all. But I know he does not hate you, Lucky. I think he—" She shook her head and looked off to the side.

It was Lucky's turn to look into Brigitte's eyes and hold her gaze. "You think he what?"

"I think he is . . . afraid. Afraid not of *you*, but of being a father, being responsible. He fears for you to love him because if you do, he will have to love you back. So he is acting in a way that will make you not want to love him." She raised a shoulder. "It is not your fault that he is this way. Do you understand that, Lucky?"

Even though she still had plenty of questions, Lucky sort of did understand. She nodded and touched her necklace, and for the first time in her life, she felt sorry for her father. After a while Brigitte got to her feet and reached for Lucky's hands, pulling her up. Then they stood leaning against each other, looking down the hill at their little town of Hard Pan.

31. a goofy smile

While Brigitte went to help the Captain, Lucky cut around behind the guests to Short Sammy's water tank house, which was wearing a garland of balloons tied to a rope completely encircling the top. It smelled like a good mixture of metal, dog, bacon grease, and Sammy. Lucky felt both hungry and not hungry for explanations; reasons why she should be happy, but wasn't.

The front door was firmly shut, so she made her way to a rear window, which was a square hole cut into the tin, and peered inside. Sammy had his back to her, but she could see he was bending over his little table, rubbing something onto the paws of a small dog who lay there on its side. Hearing or sensing her, the dog raised its head and looked right at her, smiling a goofy dog-smile that Lucky had seen before. She had seen that dog-smile often on a photograph in a sardine-can frame, hanging from a nail on Sammy's wall.

It was Roy. The dog that saved Sammy's life and got bit on the scrotum by a rattlesnake. Sammy, who blamed himself for the injury, had pledged to quit drinking if Roy were to get well, and Roy did recover because he was given the antivenom in time. But Sammy's wife had walked out on him, and she had taken Roy with her. And as far as Lucky knew, Sammy had never seen Roy again until today.

But why had Roy been out on the highway, so far from where Sammy's ex-wife lived in Sierra City?

Suddenly Sammy, too, turned his head and locked eyes with Lucky. "Well," he said.

Realizing that she'd been caught peering into Sammy's house without his knowing it, Lucky improvised. "I was looking . . . ," she began.

"Who are you looking for, man? Someone in here?" Sammy gestured toward the empty round room. He sounded mad.

"I was in big trouble and I needed you," she said. Even to her, her voice sounded wrong. It sounded accusing.

Sammy gathered the dog in his arms, straightened up

slowly, and came to the window opening. He looked into Lucky's eyes. She studied the uneven edge of the cutout window. He should tack up screens. All the pests in the

162

world could come in those openings and bother him. Lucky kicked a rock against the tin wall of his house.

"I'm sorry, man. Been kind of busy. Are you okay now? What happened?"

Lucky sighed deeply. "Oh, Miles told me the story of the lost brooch and I was looking for it and got trapped. But I made it out and I'm fine. I guess."

"Oh, man, you didn't climb down into that well, did you? Oh, hell, Lucky, you did." Sammy shook his head. "Brigitte know about it?"

"More or less, yeah."

"How'd Lincoln get you out? It *was* Lincoln, wasn't it?"

Lucky folded her arms up against the corrugated metal wall and rested her forehead on them. She spoke looking down at the ground. "Hauled me up in his net. I thought it wouldn't work and I'd crash through and fall and break every bone in my body."

163

"You didn't trust *Lincoln*? He knows more about knots and nets than Miles knows about cookies. He'd never do anything risky when it comes to that kind of operation."

Lucky didn't answer. She knew he was right. Sammy mentioning trust ignited a sudden little fire of shame in her heart and sent the heat of it to her face.

Sammy sighed. "Poor old Roy." His voice wasn't mad any longer. It sounded sad. "Sometimes we get this great gift, man, and we just take it for granted. We only figure it out, how much we lost, when it's gone."

Lucky felt like sobbing and kicking rocks at the same time. She reached through the opening and touched Roy's small head. She didn't mention that she knew all about Roy and what he had done for Sammy.

"Is he going to die?" she asked.

"Well, yeah. We all are. But not yet; we still have time. He sure wanted to be home with me. What about you, man? Have you found whatever you've been looking for?"

"Are you talking about Lincoln or Paloma?" Lucky couldn't be sure of anything. She wanted to be only six, like Miles, so she wouldn't have to face all these complicated situations.

"You tell me, man." Short Sammy shifted Roy's weight, carefully supporting the dog's body.

Lucky was silent, and after a moment Sammy said, "Roy walked a long way to find me. He can't explain why, but me and him, we both understand." Sammy looked out past Lucky for a moment, as if seeing all those miles of highway Roy had traveled. "You have to pay attention. It's not as easy with people, man, but it's possible." Sammy turned away from her. He lowered Roy gently onto a pile of old towels and T-shirts, a Sammy-smelling makeshift bed for his dog.

Lucky went to find her friends.

32. lincoln and paloma

The party was getting underway. All the Hard Panners were there, plus the group Miles called the 'ologists: the seismologist, sedimentologist, paleontologist, and mineralogist, all talking and eating stew. Pete and Brigitte were bending over their bowls, murmuring together. Brigitte laughed her deep, throaty laugh, smiling at Lucky as she slipped past them.

Paloma and HMS Beagle looked up from their stew as Lucky collapsed on an ancient wooden folding chair with INYO COUNTY, CA stenciled on its back. When Paloma offered a shy little smile, Lucky reached over and took hold of her wrist.

Paloma said, "Are you taking my pulse, or what?"

"Yeah. It's like I can feel the beating of your heart," Lucky said, and added, "Which, it's good."

"Meaning what, no cholesterol?"

"No, just it. Your heart. It's good."

"And?"

"Well, Brigitte says I should listen to you next time there's danger. I gotta try to remember that. I don't think there ever *will* be danger, but just in case, if there is any, could you please be here and remind me to pay attention? I promise, next time I'll listen."

HMS Beagle gave her bowl a last lick and then gazed lovingly at Paloma, her polite way of asking for more.

"I'll be here," Paloma said. "For one thing, I still haven't learned to swim in that bucket."

Lucky laughed. "Right. We have to work on that."

Paloma said, "Looks like I need to get more stew for the Beag. But first I'm checking *your* pulse." They switched, so that Paloma held Lucky's wrist, her fringed droopy eyes full of concentration. "Hmmm," she said.

"What?"

"In my professional opinion, you have a very good heart too, Luck. Big and strong and good. I'll be back." And she headed toward the bathtub, followed closely by HMS Beagle.

* * *

Lincoln sat on one end of an old knocked-down phone pole log that had been placed a ways apart from the party, a little up the hill, near a large creosote shrub. There was plenty of room on the pole, and Lucky plopped down smack in the center of it. Lincoln did not look at her.

"So," Lucky said. "Hi."

Lincoln leaned forward, elbows on knees, chin in hands, and gazed off to his left.

Lucky said to the back of his head, "Paloma told me how cool your pulley system was. The way you used that old tire rim. I wish I'd paid attention and seen how it worked."

More silence from Lincoln. Lucky sighed.

"Lincoln," she began, "we're supposed to be best friends."

Lincoln studied his hands. They were empty.

Lucky picked at a sliver of the phone pole log. "This whole seat is full of splinters waiting to poke us," she said. "You have to be careful."

"I know."

"I mean, I got one splinter already today." Lucky examined her hand again in the fading light.

"Yeah."

"But it doesn't really hurt. Mostly I was hurt*ful*." She turned to him. "It's weird, but I actually just realized today that it's worse to *be* hurtful than to get hurt."

Lincoln nodded, still without looking at her.

"Where is the hammock, anyway? Where's your practicing cord?" Lucky couldn't remember ever seeing Lincoln without some cord nearby. She jumped to her feet. "I hate this! You're barely talking to me just because I tried to ruin your net and then didn't trust you to save my life and then was mean to you after you *did* save my life?"

Lincoln frowned up at Lucky. "I don't get you," he said.

Tears came to her eyes. With her heel she gouged out a little hollow under the creosote. "It's just like Roy," she explained. "His whole life was a great gift, only Sammy let him go and it was almost too late. You have to pay attention to things like that."

Lincoln looked confused. "Who's Roy?" he asked. "What are you talking about?"

"You," Lucky said, before she could think about it. She swiped the corners of her eyes with her sleeve. "I finally figured it out. I was a . . . I was a real jerk." She tried to think of what she really wanted to say to Lincoln. "Listen, Lincoln, it's like I was a planet and suddenly I got out of orbit. Like I went sailing off on my own, without the sun and the moon and the other planets, without you, Lincoln, and it was awful. I thought I could zoom around on my own or just with Paloma but it was too lonely and stupid and mean and tragic."

Lincoln looked at her with his soft brown eyes.

Lucky kept trying. "You're the *link*, Lincoln. It's your first syllable, right there in your name! Knots are the links that repair the cuts, and tie things together, like your rescue net."

She paused. There was the sound of laughter from the party. Lucky plucked a sprig off the creosote. She continued, "So, so, listen. Could you do me a really big favor? It's important. Could you please, please, please tie some knots? And, um." The air filled with the spicy scent of the shrub as she pinched off one tiny waxy leaf and then another. She rubbed the branch lightly against her neck, as if it were perfume, a strong, clean fragrance to replace the musty underground odor that was still clinging to her. In a quiet, serious voice, Lucky went on, "And, oh, wait. There's one other thing. Could you, Lincoln, maybe please forgive me?"

He pressed his lips together. Then he said, "Yeah, I guess, okay." After a moment he added, "Listen. The hammock is for you."

Lucky felt something like a surge in her heart, a powerful zap that made her light-headed and unable to speak. She sat beside him on the pole.

"My friend in the International Guild of Knot Tyers thinks it's pretty much like the one Charles Darwin had in his cabin onboard the *HMS Beagle*," Lincoln said, "except his was made of canvas. I could rig some hooks in your trailer and you could hang it up for an extra bed when Paloma comes over." He hesitated, and then added, "If you want."

Lucky nodded. She sat motionless, overcome. It was a perfect, splendid, magnificent gift. She thought there couldn't possibly be any words to show what she was feeling, and then she found two small ones that would have to do. "Thank you," she said.

Lincoln smiled at her. "Happy birthday," he said. "You're gonna love being eleven."

"I know," Lucky said. "Lincoln, I'm just so glad you're . . . what you are."

"A knot tyer?"

"Yeah, but it's not just that you know how to tie knots. You know which knots to tie, and when, and why. If those contest people really see into the heart of things, you're going to win for sure. I want that so much." And it was true, even though Lucky knew it meant Lincoln would go to England. She really did want him to win.

"Well," he said, "I'm still learning." He pulled a cord from his pocket, held one end of it steady, and looped the other end over and around and under and through. His hands, Lucky noticed, were long-fingered, the knuckles well-defined, almost like the hands of a man.

33. one way to see stars in l.a.

It was getting dark when Paloma, with bowls of stew in each hand, made her way to the phone pole and sat on Lucky's other side. "Here," she said. "You two must be starved. It's the best Bathtub Stew I ever had, which, it's so good I bet even my dad will like it."

It was kind of weird to see Mr. and Mrs. Wellborne laughing and talking with all the Old Desert Rat Characters, sipping from their spoons and admiring Short Sammy's festivated water tank house. Sammy himself had finally emerged, Roy under his arm, each of them grinning. Lucky knew they were both okay when Sammy repositioned his stained cowboy hat at a certain angle, which meant he was about to launch into one of the old Hard Pan legends. Miles, his hair and skin glinting golden in the light of the thick bed of embers underneath the bathtub, seemed to be emitting light and heat himself, like a little sun.

Lucky thought she'd never been so hungry in her life. She

wasn't even aware of the others as she ate, as the rich, hot broth and tender chunks of meat and vegetables filled up the empty, ravenous place inside her. She and Lincoln finished at the same time, upending their bowls to drink the last drops.

"Wow," Lincoln said.

"Mmmm," Lucky agreed.

"Everyone's having a good time," Paloma said. "I don't think my parents have worried once since they got here. It's like a miracle."

"When I went down there for cupcakes earlier, your dad told me they decided this is a great town for kids," Lincoln said to her. "Everybody looks out for everybody else, and there are none of those dangers and temptations that city kids encounter all the time."

The two of them turned to look at Lucky, who said, "Um." They all three laughed, and then Lucky added, "Well, he's kind of right, after all."

"But then," Lincoln continued, "as we're talking and he's showing me the Hummer, he looks up and his whole face changes. He gets this expression on his face, half horrified and half amazed. I turn around and right behind me is the burro, the old one that came into Hard Pan the other night, just standing there close enough to touch. 'Don't tell Mrs. Wellborne,' he says to me. 'A wild animal! She'll worry.' So I promised to keep Chesterfield a secret."

"Someone better tell Chesterfield," Lucky said, stacking her bowl and Lincoln's to the side. "There he is, down at the end of the path, eating Sammy's greasewood plant."

Lincoln said, "Klincke Ken told me that he must have been someone's pet and escaped or was let free, because he isn't afraid of humans at all. He allowed Miles to go right up to him and pet him. Turns out Klincke Ken had a burro himself, years ago, and he taught her to open the refrigerator, but he said she could never learn to close it."

Paloma said, "Greasewood. Yum."

That would have normally got Lucky going, but she was too wrung out for a serious laughing jag. She stretched her arms and eased herself down until her butt reached the ground, and then she lay on her back, legs up on the pole. Then Lincoln and Paloma eased themselves back too. It was comfortable, with their legs resting on the pole, six shoes lined up, Lincoln's seeming gigantic next to the girls'. They cradled their heads to look at the stars, at the vastness of everything.

"Are all the cupcakes gone?"

"Yeah, but Brigitte kept some extras for us at home."

"The only time I saw this many stars," Paloma said, "was after we had an earthquake in L.A. It was the scariest thing in my life. Which, the whole house jerked and rocked, it felt like forever. The power went off; it was pitch-dark. My dad said we should go outside while he checked for gas leaks. The neighbors were out there too, wearing their pajamas."

"You went out and looked at stars?"

"Well, not for that reason, at first, but just to see if everyone else's power was out and if anyone needed help. And electricity in the whole *city* was out. So we were all really excited and happy, like at this party, because no one in the neighborhood had gotten hurt, or had any real damage in their houses. Anyway, I just kind of looked up, which, it was amazing. Wall-to-wall stars. Usually you don't even bother to look for stars, because there are only maybe a dozen."

"So why were there so many stars that night?"

"At first I actually thought it was because of the earthquake, that somehow it made an opening in the smog or the ozone or the clouds or something. And I thought, well, it's almost worth it, an earthquake scaring you out of your wits, if it means you get to see the sky like this. But then I heard the neighbors saying it was because all the lights of the city were off. Turns out it's light pollution that keeps us from seeing the stars."

"That only happens here when there's a full moon," Lucky said, "and then the light is so bright you can read by it. Most other nights we have the world's best view of our galaxy."

HMS Beagle appeared, tail wagging. She licked a corner of Lucky's forehead, turned around three times, and flopped to the ground nearby. Lucky breathed in the deeply comfortable scent of her fur.

"Oh," Lincoln said. "By the way, I solved the mystery of the universe."

Lucky smiled to herself. "Good," she said. "I've been waiting."

"Okay," Lincoln began. "Lift up your head for a second." Lucky did, and Lincoln extended his right arm underneath it. "Say I'm the Milky Way. I'm a spiral galaxy with five arms."

"Come on," Paloma said, laughing.

"Seriously," Lincoln answered. "My five arms extend out, each curving in the same direction. *This* arm"—he bent the right one at the elbow and at the wrist to show the spiral curve—"has the solar system at its tip, like at the end of my finger."

Turning her head, Lucky felt the muscle of Lincoln's arm under it and saw his hand curving out and over her.

"See?" said Lincoln softly. "My fingertip is far away from my core, but still connected to me."

"Whoa," Paloma murmured.

There was a sudden lull. The party was beginning to end. All three of them looked up at the stars again, at their galaxy, the Milky Way. Lucky felt the earth under her back, pebbly and cool, and thought about how the world was spinning and flying through space, around and around the sun, like the most fabulous ride in the universe, vast and eternal. And every day she got to be on that wild ride, which mostly she didn't even notice, except when she had a best friend on each side and gazillions of stars overhead to remind her. It was a moment in time of such grandeur and overpoweringness that it almost hurt.

"Linc," said Lucky. She couldn't say any more. She finally felt linked, they were all linked, Miles to his mom, Brigitte to America, Sammy to Roy, the Wellbornes to Hard Pan, the burro to the town, the Earth to its galaxy, she to her two best friends.

Pal and Linc and Luck.

acknowledgments

For sharing experiences and information about their burros, many thanks to Ginny Freeman and Kathy Edmonston; and to Terri Farley for making the introductions. Thanks to Jim Hays (aka Turtle Jim) for extraordinary true stories of his jenny, Sally, and for responding to my depiction of Chesterfield. Thanks to Fern Henry for candor about the behavior of the herd next door. Wild or feral burros, mostly descended from the Old West miners' donkeys, are highly intelligent, highly adapted animals. Any errors of fact in the text regarding these wonderful creatures are mine alone.

For information on the burro adoption program of the Bureau of Land Management, see blm.gov/wo/st/en/prog/wild_horses_and_burro.html. Or visit the website of the largest donkey rescue center in the United States: donkeyrescue.org.

Grateful appreciation, again, to members of the International Guild of Knot Tyers (igkt.net) for their responsiveness to my questions, especially Lindsey Philpott and Barry Brown, who helped untangle all the knotty problems this novice knot-tying author encountered. If I have slipped in any knotting descriptions, it is due to my own poor technique—despite their always knowledgeable advice. Please note that the contest Lincoln enters is fictional; in reality, there is no such contest sponsored by the IGKT.

Des Pawson MBE, Museum of Knots and Sailors' Ropework, and Peter McGrath of the HMS Beagle Project (the beagleproject.com) kindly verified details of Charles Darwin's actual hammock and of his cabin aboard the *HMS Beagle*.

Geoffrey Budworth's books on knot tying are among the most alluring and handsome available. His *Knots: Get to Grips with Knotting Know-How* (Sterling, 2003) is a fine introduction. Mr. Budworth, cofounder of the International Guild of Knot Tyers, graciously consented to my including him as a character in this story.

Grateful appreciation to Andrew Kirk of the Inyo County Department of Environmental Health Services for clarifying the stipulation in the California code that will plague Brigitte in times to come. (Readers, please stay tuned.)

Thank you, once again, Joe and Jody Bruce.

I'm indebted again to the following early readers for their kind and useful suggestions: Eva and Nadia Mitnick, Virginia Walter, Theresa Nelson, Lucy Frank, Georgia and Steven Chun, Erin Miskey, and Eva Cox, who asked about Roy.

For her integrity and thoughtfulness, thanks always to Susan Cohen at Writers House.

Enormous thanks to Matt Phelan for the humanity and generosity of spirit that shows in every stroke of his pens, pencils, and brushes.

I'd still be at the bottom of the abandoned well were it not for the support and guidance of my brilliant editor Ginee Seo. Profound thanks to her and to Jordan Brown for giving me the light to write by when I was in that dark place.

Special appreciation to everyone at Atheneum for their extraordinary support, expertise, and attention to detail. You remind me, always, of how lucky I truly am.

Dick Jackson, you may not know it but you sang to me throughout the writing of this book: spirituals, hymns, anthems, and ballads. Your voice will always be in my ears.

For moral support, heartfelt thanks to my sweet sisters Patricia Leavengood and Georgia Chun; and to my splendid beloved Ernie Nortap.

to the reader

Brain Surgery for Beginners and Other Operations for Minors, Miles's new favorite book, is by Steve Parker, illustrated and designed by David West (Millbrook, 1995).

Bathtub Stew is described in James Austin Wilder's *Jack-Knife Cookery* (Dutton, 1929), along with many other inventive ways of cooking outdoors.

The Ashley Book of Knots (Doubleday, 1944) is available in book form and as a searchable CD.

*

*

Here's a sneak peek
at the conclusion
to Susan Patron's
Newbery Medal–winning trilogy!

*

*

LUCKY for GOOD

Coming April 2011

Ollie Martin

Nobody sat on the splintery unroofed official bus stop bench in front of Sierra City Elementary. Instead, the Hard Pan kids and the Dale kids waited nearby for Sandi the bus driver on a low, wide concrete wall. It was a handy, convenient wall for hanging around on—you could straddle it, face-to-face with another person, to have a private conversation, or you could lie on it and gaze up into the leafy ceiling of a cottonwood tree. But if you sat facing front in the normal way, like on a regular bus stop bench, you would be staring at your future: Einstein Jr. High, right across the street. Everything about Einstein worried Lucky, from its name (which made you think you had to be a genius to go there) to its student population. Those students were all bigger and older and what Paloma called, in one of their many discussions of the pitfalls and dangers of junior high, more experienced.

On that warm May afternoon, two girls from Dale

straddled the wall knee-to-knee, playing a fast hand-clapping game; Miles organized his dinosaur trading cards; and Lucky lay on her back, reading a book about the love aspect of Charles Darwin's life. She hoped Lincoln would hurry up; he was discussing with Ms. Baum-Izzart a project he wanted to get school credit for during his summer in England. If the project was about nooses, Lincoln should not emphasize that aspect to the principal, in Lucky's private opinion. Nooses were just knots to Lincoln—well, as he'd explained, not *just* knots, but very special, specific knots that had to be done right the first time—but a principal would probably be creeped out about the *idea* of nooses and not understand his interest in the technical aspect. As Lucky thought about this, she noticed a boy running across the street, heading toward them. He carried a skateboard.

Lucky was surprised to see that it was the nephew who had been in Stu Burping's truck at the town meeting. When he got to the curb, he threw the skateboard down, jumped on, and spun it around. Then he leaped the curb, got up speed, reversed direction, and made the board spring up into the air, as if it were glued to his feet. The board landed on its side, so the underneath was visible; like the top, it was decorated with elaborate, colorful designs. And written on it in multicolored puffy-graffiti letters was the name Ollie Martin.

"Hey, I need to practice some tricks on that wall," he called out, flipping the board up with the toe of his sneaker. "You guys clear off."

The Dale girls, who were third graders, swung their legs over and moved obediently to one side. But Miles looked up from his trading cards and said, "This is *our* school's wall."

"Well, no," Ollie Martin said with mock patience and mock friendliness. "Right now, that wall is *my* wall."

"Look," Lucky said, "the bus'll be here in a minute and then you can have it all to yourself."

The skater rocked his board, clacking the pavement, and pulled a stick of Juicy Fruit from his pocket. "Oh, right," he said conversationally, like they were just old friends shooting the breeze, "the bus that goes," he paused, smiled, and threw the gum wrapper on the ground, "to the *outlying areas*." He said "outlying areas" in a sarcastic way that stung Lucky, as if underneath that official teacher phrase lurked some awful meaning.

"Just Dale and Hard Pan," Miles explained.

"Oh! Just Dale and Hard Pan," the boy repeated, still with that fake niceness, as if *he* knew so much more, as if they were babies. He smacked his Juicy Fruit. It was becoming more than Lucky could bear.

She said, "So, *Ollie*, were you actually named for a skateboard trick or what?"

Ollie Martin didn't hear the little jab of irony in Lucky's voice, or if he did, he chose to ignore it. "Actually, yeah," he said. "My dad was a world-class skateboarder." Everyone stared at him; you couldn't top that for dad coolness. This annoyed Lucky further; Ollie was just plain showing off. He pulled out another stick of gum and peered down the street—no bus was coming—then made a sweeping gesture that clearly meant *get off the wall now*. Lucky ignored this; she turned to the next page in her book. Miles stacked his cards.

Ollie narrow-eyed Lucky, dropping the second wadded-up gum wrapper onto the ground. He flipped his board up in the air, caught it, and examined the underside, as if to double-check his own name. He said, "I've been to Hard Pan. That's where some illegal immigrant got busted by the health department." He nodded, agreeing with himself. "Everyone's heard about that, because, like, the whole town is full of trailer trash and welfare losers. Same kind of people made my dad lose his job." Ollie whacked the board hard against his thigh, sending the wheels spinning. "So this woman opens a restaurant and what was that specialty on the menu?" Ollie didn't ask this as if he expected an answer. He asked, Lucky knew, because he wanted to answer it himself. "Oh, yeah, ground-up ratburgers. Just add a lotta garlic, and they say it tastes almost like chicken."

"What is *wrong* with you? Shut *up*," Lucky said, but she knew she couldn't make him, and Ollie Martin knew it too. He wore skateboard scrapes and road rash on his big-boned arms and a be-cool expression on his face.

Ollie rolled his eyes, signaling he was out of patience. "Listen, children, this is wasting my time. Why don't you two go play over there with the other little girls."

Lucky blazed, as if she'd been set on fire. "We are not children!" she shouted, even though they *were*, of course, children. What she really meant was *quit acting like you're better than us!* He gave her his little gum-smacking smile, and she yelled, "Get out of here big, red-nosed creepo!" Not a very good insult, but it was all she could think of.

"I know who you are. I saw you." Ollie moved close to Lucky, looming over her; he smelled like gum and the oil on his skateboard wheels. "You were with the ratburger lady. I heard the county got there just in time before she poisoned the whole town."

Suddenly Lucky clambered up so she was standing on the wall. Now she was taller than him. "Yeah, I was with her, and don't call her that. She happens to be my mother and she's a professional chef, and she cooks better than you can even *imagine*, so back off!"

Instead of backing off, though, Ollie smiled again in his cool, horrid, junior-high way, as if he'd just scored a point. "Oh, give me a break. Tell her, fine, be a professional chef but stay in her own country instead of coming here and putting Americans out of a job. Come on, figure it out; it's not that complicated. She's working the system."

Lucky didn't know exactly what this meant, but it sounded bad and insulting. She said, "She's a naturalized American citizen!"

Ollie ignored this. He added yet another stick of gum to the wad in his mouth, flicking the crumbled wrapper toward Lucky. "So where's your father? I bet you don't have a clue."

Maybe because it was a question she could not answer or

because she was sick of Ollie Martin's attitude, and sick of the way he made Hard Pan seem like a dump, and sick of how he attacked Brigitte without even *knowing* her, and sick of his *gum*. So, without realizing it, she drew her hand drew back and then rammed forward with a mighty force, punching him on the jaw. She felt the impact of it all the way to her shoulder and heard a hard thud, like a bag of wet sand dropped on the ground. Then her arm was being yanked hard behind her. She was shoved down and pushed onto her stomach, her cheek raking the dirt.

"You little—" Ollie held her down, ramming a knee in her back. But suddenly it stopped. Ollie was off her, there was shouting, and she sucked in air, trembling uncontrollably, not sure, as she got on all fours, if her muscles would allow her to stand. Her knuckles burned, as if they had skidded on concrete; her legs shook as she swayed on her hands and knees. She felt like throwing up.

And then many things were happening at once. It was hard to pay attention, hard to focus, because Lucky was filled with a powerful urge, if only she could get to her feet, to go roaring after Ollie Martin and pound him, *pummel* him with her fists. But she was scared, too, because she knew now how strong he was. And seething hot anger spurted through her veins because he was so wrong about her mother, but—and this made her more infuriated—right about her father.

And finally she was sitting on the wall, spitting out dirt, and Sandi the bus driver's voice was nearby, with the static of her two-way radio. Sandi saying, ". . . ambulance at the Sierra City Elementary bus stop. A kid is hurt."

Then Lucky felt a rich gladness wash through her: It was okay. She was apparently injured but would live, and Ollie Martin would get in deep, deep trouble for hurting her.

But when she checked herself, Lucky found out she was not the one who had been hurt, except for her feelings and her pride. It was Lincoln, propped against the wall, his face white and filled with pain, cradling his right arm to his chest.

"Get back, Miles. Move away!" Sandi shouted. "I need a clear path here."

Lucky watched as Miles picked something up, scooted out of the way, and came to sit on the ground between Lincoln and Lucky.

"I don't get why that boy Ollie hates us so much," he said, frowning up at Lucky. "But you shouldn't have socked him. You'll probably have to go to hell for that." He swiped the back of an arm across his eyes, and glared at her.

"No, she won't," Lincoln said, his voice strained.

Lucky was still a little breathless, as if she'd almost drowned. "Oh, Miles," she said. "It'll be okay."

As the ambulance pulled up, she glanced down at Miles. Arms wrapped around legs, forehead on knees, and his lips, Lucky could see, silently moving. And clinched in one fist, she saw what he had been carefully gathering up from the ground: a handful of Juicy Fruit gum wrappers. ❄✳

For fun. For inspiration. For you.
Atheneum.

The Secret Language of Girls
by Frances O'Roark Dowell

Kira-Kira
by Cynthia Kadohata

The Higher Power of Lucky
by Susan Patron

Beneath My Mother's Feet
by Amjed Qamar

Standing for Socks
by Elissa Brent Weissman

Here's How I See It—
Here's How It Is
by Heather Henson

Atheneum Books for Young Readers • Published by Simon & Schuster

IRRESISTABLE FICTION
from Edgar Award—winning author
FRANCES O'ROARK DOWELL!

DOVEY COE

THE SECRET
LANGUAGE OF GIRLS

THE KIND OF FRIENDS
WE USED TO BE

WHERE I'D LIKE TO BE

CHICKEN BOY

SHOOTING THE MOON

Finn Garrett is disappearing.

He used to have black hair and skin-colored skin, but each day his hair gets whiter and his skin gets more transparent. It's been happening since the day his father died. He can't figure out how to stop it. But before he vanishes completely, he's writing everything down for us, his faithful readers. In words and pictures, these are the memoirs of the Last Invisible Boy.

"Heartbreaking and uplifting . . . a gutsy book that will stay with me a long time."   —JEFF KINNEY, author of *Diary of a Wimpy Kid*

The Last Invisible Boy by Evan Kuhlman
From Atheneum Books for Young Readers
Published by Simon & Schuster
KIDS.SimonandSchuster.com
EBOOK EDITION ALSO AVAILABLE

From two-time Newbery Medalist
E. L. Konigsburg

e. l. konigsburg

The View from Saturday

e. l. konigsburg

e. l. konigsburg

Jennifer, Hecate, Macbeth, William McKinley, and me, Elizabeth

e. l. konigsburg

(george)

e. l. konigsburg

About the B'nai Bagels

e. l. konigsburg

Journey to an 800 Number

e. l. konigsburg

The Mysterious Edge of the Heroic World

From Atheneum
Published by Simon & Schuster